DEDICATION
To working stuff out.

Books by Zoe Dawson

Romantic Comedy

Going to the Dogs Series
Leashed
Groomed for Murder
Hounded
Collared
Fetched (companion novella to Hounded)
Handled (companion novella to Groomed for Murder)
Tangled (companion novella to Leashed)
Captured (companion novella to Collared)

New Adult

Brave (Christmas novella)

Hope Parish Novels

A Perfect Secret Series
A Perfect Mess
A Perfect Mistake
A Perfect Dilemma

Novellas
Finally Again
Beauty Shot
Mark Me

Urban Fantasy

The Starbuck Chronicles
AfterLife

Erotica

Forbidden Plays Series – Erotic Shorts
Monster Man
Hot Read
Illegal Motions

A PERFECT WEDDING

BLUE
MOON
CREATIVE
LLC

write ∗ paint ∗ create

Find Zoe Dawson on the web!
www.zoedawson.com

Cover design by Zoe Dawson
Editing Services provided by Faith Freewoman

ISBN: 978-0-9909075-7-2

ACKNOWLEDGMENTS

I'd like to thank Sue Stewart and Leisha O'Quinn for reading this book and giving me great feedback. Thank you, also, to Faith Freewoman for her excellent advice and editing skills. A big thank you also to Jessica Allain for her excellent Photoshop skills.

CHAPTER ONE

Booker

"HELLO."

"Book."

"Boone. Do you know what time it is?" My voice was rusty from disuse and exhaustion.

"Yeah, and if you weren't setting off my tripdar, I'd be asleep instead of on the phone."

"I'm not—"

"Huckleberry...you are. Has to be you. Brax is drunk with happiness, Ma beams every time I see her. My kid is drooling and giggling all the time, and Verity.... Well, let's just say she has no complaints. So it has to be you. Because I usually can't sleep when it's you. When it's Brax, I lose my appetite. Go figure. Now, what the hell is up? Is Breebree okay?"

I didn't know what to tell my brother. Aubree had been so caught up in everything she thought she needed to do, I scarcely saw her. It was just one month till our wedding, and I'd never seen her that stressed before. I ached with the need to do something to help her, but decided staying out of her way would be easiest on her.

Work was important. Of course it was. I had been getting stuff done right and left, even had a blast signing at a conference in downtown New Orleans the previous week.

Which Aubree had to miss because of school and her volunteer job. She'd been upset, visibly upset, and tired enough to just drop her head in her hand and give me the opportunity to hold her through it. I chafed at her constant and overwhelming commitments, but didn't feel free to complain, because she was working her tail off for the common good. How could I argue with that?

She told me often this was the way it was going to be. That we had to suck it up and power forward. Before the phone rang, I was lying here at four in the morning trying to figure out how I was going to manage it for our married life. We'd been living in New Orleans going on eight months, and I'd spent most of that time getting only bits and pieces of my gorgeous redhead.

It didn't help that I'd spent most of yesterday calling Aubree several times and texting her with no response. And then worrying about her silence. She was probably caught up in studying, but I couldn't be sure, and as the night wore on, I got angry about it.

But it was an impotent sort of anger. Because I needed to be understanding. She was under a lot of pressure...with the wedding, her studies—her honking big stressor was organic chemistry—and her volunteer work. I spent more time worrying about Aubree than thinking about anything else. She pushed herself too hard, and I was stressed about her, about our relationship, and about our future.

And, dammit, I needed...something. Some concession, some options.

"Your Breebree is stressed out, but she isn't here right now and hasn't responded to my calls or texts all day, so I'm a little worried. She's most likely studying."

There was complete silence on the other line, then Boone sighed, "Booker, I know you love that girl, but you need to be honest with yourself and with her."

"What is that supposed to mean?"

"I know you. When times get tough and you get stressed, you tend to deny your feelings."

"Really, Boone? How are you this articulate so early in the morning?"

"I don't want to tell you."

"Why?"

"I don't want to rub it in your face."

"Rub what?"

"I'm so incredibly happy...I...I sometimes pinch myself to make sure it's real. Since River cleared our name, it's still not perfect, but I feel and see a difference. Ever since Brax found out about Daddy, it's been better. Sad, though. Ma is more than willing to talk about it, and I find that I want to listen now. She's doing great, by the way and Mr. Sut...Win is good for her. Why don't you come home for a bit? We'll get drunk and leave Brax in the bayou. That'll be good for a laugh."

"You've got to come up with something better than that."

"Oh, didn't I mention he would be naked and in a tree?"

I chuckled in spite of myself.

Boone snickered softly and I heard a door close. "That would *definitely* be worth a laugh."

"I don't know."

"We'll pump iron, eat junk food, play video games, and do other manly things."

I laughed again. "Isn't that counterproductive?

Eating junk and pumping iron? Don't they cancel each other out?"

"Geez, you're making me pull out the big guns. Okay, here it is. I've got juicy gossip and red Gummy Bears, too."

"I admit defeat."

"Sweet! I'll see you when you get here. Now I'm going to see if my wife is awake."

"You mean you're going to wake her up."

"She can't resist me, even this early." Boone chuckled and hung up.

And a surge of jealousy shredded me. I couldn't remember the last time I had jumped Aubree's bones, or she'd jumped mine. Hell, even touched, cuddled—anything. I was bored as hell, and ordinary wasn't why I'd chosen to be with Aubree.

The longer I lay there stewing the worse my frustration got. Even a nice guy like me had a breaking point.

I heard the key in the lock, and in spite of my impotent anger and my unmet needs, I was relieved. She was all right, and the love I had bottled up also surged to the surface. We so needed to have some fun together...even if it was just an evening of movies and popcorn—and bones-jumping, of course. It would help a lot.

I couldn't go on like this, especially not since it would be years before she became the doctor of a small sleepy town and finally had time for me. Or would she have time for me even then?

When the door closed and I heard her making a concerted effort to stay quiet, I said. "I'm awake." Damn, I loved that about her. She was so considerate.

"Oh, I'm sorry. Did I wake you up?" She sounded tired, and I got a pang in my chest. Too much working too hard and not having enough leisure time. Time to be with me and unwind.

"I've been awake," I said, sitting up in bed, the sheet dropping away from my bare chest. I draped my arms over my knees. *And that is your fault, my beautiful.*

"Couldn't sleep?" Her sleepy eyes went over me, slowly and I had to take a breath. Those were definitely bones-jumping vibes I was getting. But, she looked so freaking tired. Who was I kidding? I wanted to jump her bones anyway, tired or not.

"No. Too many ideas running around in my monkey brain." I was getting hard from the way she was looking at me. "Hey, I was thinking maybe you and I could plan to have dinner tonight."

"Tonight?" Her voice was so eager, it warmed me all the way to my toes. She reached into her Einstein tote and dug out her phone. She turned it on and stared at it.

Her green eyes popped up to mine, and she made a face that told me she was upset all over again. "Ohmigod. I missed three calls and five texts! Shoot, babe. I'm sorry. I turned off my phone when I was meeting with my o-chem professor, and I forgot to turn it back on. I hope you weren't worried...wait...oh damn...is that why you're awake?"

"Partly," I said.

She sighed. "I feel like I haven't seen you in weeks. The end of the semester sucks."

"It definitely does," I said. "Ah, so, tonight...dinner?"

"Right," she gave me a depreciating smile. "What would I do without you?" She tapped her phone repeatedly, then her shoulders slumped. She dropped her head back and said, low and fierce. "Oh, *fuuuccckkkk* no!" she shouted.

I sat up straighter. Aubree never said that word. Well almost never. "Sugar, babe..."

"I have a sorority meeting tonight, which has already

been rescheduled three times...ah...because of me. So I can't tonight. Why didn't you tie me down when I mused over the fact there were too few sororities for pre-med students and none on Tulane's campus?"

"Because my sassy redhead has a mind of her own and I'm a little scared of you."

She laughed. "No you're not, even if I've been, in the past, labelled as a ballbuster."

"That was *not* me."

"I have three suspects, all their names begin with a B, and, ladies and gentlemen of the jury, they're all Outlaws."

"I will not be a snitch, and you can't break me."

"Oh, is that so? I can break you, Booker Thomas Outlaw, and don't you forget it."

I laughed, knowing that she could and very easily. "You got no proof, lady."

She gave me a look and I raised my brows and we both laughed.

"Okay, tomorrow night?"

"No, got another intense study group session. O-chem is killing me. I wish you were a chemistry master instead of a word master."

"Oh, babe," I said, catching my bottom lip in my mouth, leaning back and letting her see how the sheet tented my erection. "I am a chemistry master."

Her lips parted and her eyes riveted to what I like to call an impressive man moment. When a woman looks at your dick like that, yeah, punch-in-the-gut sexy. She took a soft breath, and my blood surged.

"Geezus," I said, "What does it take to get some time with you? A time machine? A gadget that slows time?" Humor was always my fallback, but I was dying here. The pressures of her schedule suffocated me. I hid my disappointment behind my comedy.

"How about that impressive time-altering, time

shattering gadget you got going there?"

I acted nonchalant as I pushed off the covers, my hard dick popping free, swung my feet to the floor and strode to my dresser. Pulling a drawer open, I grabbed a jock, a pair of socks and my running shorts, fighting a grin. "I'm going to take my nifty gadget running with me. Apparently you are much too busy for me." I turned and gave her a serious look and sighed. "I'm sure you have a full day and need to get some sleep." Guilt flooded her eyes and tugged at my heart. God, I wanted her, but she did need to sleep. She had class in three hours. Slipping on the jock, I reached for my shorts, but she grabbed my wrist.

"Oh, I don't think so," she said. "That, *gadget* isn't going anywhere, and, since it's attached to you, neither are you."

I turned to face her, huffing a laugh. "Really?" I said, snatching up my shorts and pulling away from her. "I'm not sure I want to let an 'alleged' ballbuster anywhere near my junk."

I nudged my drawer closed and opened another one, grabbing a T-shirt. I brushed past her, but she pressed her hand to my back and I stopped.

"Booker," she said softly. "Sleep is overrated. When I become a doctor, I'm going to publish an article about it. But right now, since I'm still working on that...maybe you can help me with some research."

Ah, fuck. It didn't matter how mad I got, or how charged the situation, or how much I missed her. That girl *still* got to me.

She curled her arm around my waist, and I took a breath when she pressed her body against my back.

Her fingers trailed across my abs and I sucked in an involuntary breath. "You know I can't resist you in a jock. You and your gadget look so...sexy and it's been too...long." She breathed in deep as if she was trying to take me into her body.

She teased me some more, but I didn't want to think with my dick. Sleep wasn't overrated. It was essential. Maybe a run would let me release some of the pressure in my chest and keep my brothers' tripdar from going off.

Then she delved beneath the waistband and ran her hand over the length of me. I groaned and turned, dislodging her hand, panting.

Two things I wasn't going to do. Kiss her or put my hands on her. She needed to...my brain kinda froze... ah...to...sleep.

"Booker," she said. Her face was turned up toward mine, her hand going back to the waistband of my jock. She looked down and sighed. "Sometimes I forget how beautiful you are."

"Aubree...I..." I began, but she leaned forward and kissed my chest. The T-shirt fell out of my hand. Then she ran her tongue over the curve of muscle just below my nipple, at the same time she pushed back into my jock and wrapped her hand around me, moving it gently up and down while her thumb circled the tip. I only realized I was clutching her head when the softness of her hair slipped through my fingers.

She moved lower and bit me on my ribs, and a soft sound burst out of me as tingles glided all the way down to the base of my spine and my dick.

I gave up and simply lifted her face to mine and kissed her. There was nothing to say, not right now, not when all I wanted, all I needed was to touch her, to slide my tongue into her mouth and taste her, to fill myself up with her.

Our lips met, hers parted, and a hundred emotions flooded through me. I expected pleasure, electrifying pleasure—but I also experienced relief, bone deep.

This was home. Being with Aubree, our bodies

touching. She came up on tiptoe, her mouth on mine, her arms going around my neck, and I slid my hand down her back.

Then further.

Two good intentions clobbered in under thirty seconds. I was kissing her and had my hand on her ass —and it was incredible.

This was going to get crazy, fast. Real fast. I could tell. The kiss had gone from "home sweet home" to hot and deep instantly. I tried not to stick my tongue halfway down her throat, tried not to devour her, but she was already there, and I was drowning in the love I felt—on the edge of desperation, reveling in the heat of her skin, in the all-consuming soft wetness of her mouth.

I pulled away and took a couple of quick breaths. "Are you sure about sleeping..."

"To hell with sleep. I want you, Booker, now. And, afterwards, we're going to breakfast at Café Du Monde so I can work on my love handles with many beignets."

"Why don't you get into bed?" I said, "And I'll close the curtains and light the candles.

She pulled her shirt over her head and was unzipping her skirt while I headed toward the window, since I'd forgotten to close the curtains last night while distracted with worry. My dick straining against the jock, I closed the curtains, accompanied by the rustle of sheets. I lit the candles and double-checked to be sure they weren't too close to the fabric.

As it turned out, we didn't make it to Café Du Monde, but after she fell asleep, I realized that I needed some time to think about what was gnawing at me. My brothers would say I overthought everything, but I was struggling with this...something...that was bothering me. It had to be dealt with. Boone might have the right idea. Maybe distance, being completely away from her would do it.

I went to Café Du Monde and got her some beignets and set them beside the bed. I gently pulled up the blanket over her shoulder, made sure the alarm was set so she would have time to get to class. I set my bag on the bed and packed my stuff while I watched her sleep. Before I left, I kissed her softly on her slack mouth, my heart heavy.

#

Aubree

I jerked awake as the alarm shrieked in my ears. Bolting up in bed, still feeling like I was dealing with a party bash hangover, I cleared my eyes and saw the beignets beside the bed. Dammit, the surge of regret was only eclipsed by the wash of tenderness snaking through me when I realized I had fallen asleep and hadn't been able to talk to Booker over breakfast. He was so good to me and I...was totally neglecting him. Hated it, but it was our reality.

I could tell from the quiet that Booker wasn't here. He was probably out running. I sighed, thinking about how good it had felt to touch him, make love to him, hold him. God, I missed him. I was counting the days to the end of the semester.

I got out of bed, working on punching my brain into working order. I was so groggy, had been so out of it.

When I saw the time, I grumbled. I had to be in class in an hour. I dropped my face into my hands and swallowed back tears and regrets. *Bam!* The emotion hit me like a ton of bricks. My ability to cope was at an all-time low, and I wanted to deal with all this stuff that was piling up, but was totally overwhelmed.

In the bathroom I found a used towel draped over the shower. I frowned and touched the terry. It was still damp, which meant that Booker wasn't running...then I noticed his razor and other items usually next to the sink were gone. Alarmed, I went to his closet, my insides shaky. When I didn't see his overnight bag, that shakiness turned up a notch.

He was *gone*. I mean *completely* gone. Packed his things gone. I rushed to the window and looked out, hoping his car was still there, but the Mustang was gone, too. This wasn't like Booker. I took a breath and tried to calm myself down before I called him.

I searched for my phone in my Einstein tote for five minutes before I remembered I had thrown it on the bed. When I finally unearthed it, I called him. He picked up on the first ring.

"Hey, Babe."

"Booker, where are you?"

He sighed. "On my way to Suttontowne."

"Why? Is something wrong?"

"No, everything is fine. I'm just going to see my brothers. It's no big deal."

"Are you sure? Are you upset about break—"

"No, you were tired. I understand." I leaned against the wall and closed my eyes, so sick at heart I couldn't move. He was giving me the answers he thought I wanted to hear, and I got even more worried. Booker was a complex, beautiful man, and I never wanted to downplay that, but I also knew that he wouldn't discuss anything until he was ready. No amount of pushing was going to help. He had to think it through, my brainy Outlaw. Then he said, suggestively, "Besides, I got what I wanted."

Humor was his armor. I knew that, and I laughed softly. "I know this isn't easy on you, sugar. I can try to do better."

"Hush, you have been working so hard to keep all your balls in the air. Your studies, your extracurricular activities, and your volunteer work...plus the wedding preparations. This will give you a break from having to fit me into all that."

"Booker. Do you feel that I don't want to fit you in? You're already in, and I know it's been hectic, and you are such a trooper. We're almost done with the semester. It'll get better."

"I know," he said, but I was so in tune with my man, I heard it in his voice. He was holding back, and that brought to the fore all my own doubts. Why couldn't I find a gown I liked, especially since the wedding was getting close? Way close. I had a million details to handle. River and Verity had offered, but I felt like it was my job to make sure everything was right, that everything was under control.

I wanted the wedding to be perfect. I'd dreamed since I was little about getting married and how it would be. So I wanted to handle every detail.

The push to become a doctor was consuming me. It had to. The odds against getting into medical school were grim. Fifty/fifty. And I wanted to get into Tulane so I wouldn't have to take Booker farther from his family. Once I was ready for my residency, Lafayette or New Orleans would be my main choices. But somewhere in the mix of all my organization, I'd messed up with my man, because it was clear there was something seriously wrong.

Didn't he know how much I loved him? Was I lacking there, too?

I was already worried about possibly flunking o-chem. I was having such a hard time in that class, more than any other class I'd ever taken. I couldn't seem to get it, and it was the first time it had happened to me. If I flunked organic chemistry, my dreams of becoming a doctor would go up in smoke.

I couldn't admit it to anyone. I especially couldn't tell

Booker. Because he'd probably think it was just my anxiety over perfection, my need to excel. But losing Booker wasn't an option. It was impossible. I'd do anything. A terrible tightness filled my chest and, trembling, I took a shaky breath. Totally weak in the knees.

"Babe," he said softly. "It's just a visit."

"I'm sorry about this morning and last night and all the other nights I have been busy. I think about you all the time." In all the time I'd known Booker, he had always been there for me. Always. I wanted to be there for him. He had the right to expect me to be there for him when he needed me. And I wanted to be with him, all the time, but I was caught somewhere between my lifelong passion for medicine and my all-consuming love for Booker. How was I supposed to do both and do them well? It seemed that Booker had been the one to suffer, and I hated it.

I had no idea how to fix it.

Especially if he wouldn't talk to me. I couldn't blame him. I had juggled everything poorly and dropped the ball. I could only hope our relationship wasn't made of glass.

"Aubree, go. Get ready for class and stop worrying about me. I'm going to go fool around with my dumb-ass brothers."

"That worries me more." He laughed, and the sound of it warmed me. "Promise me you won't let them talk you into something...stupid."

"I'll only say that I'll try. You know what they're like," he said with the delicious sarcastic tone that I loved so much.

I chuckled. "Yes, I do. I'll call you after I get off from work."

"All right. I love you, Aubree."

"I love you more."

It was a grim morning. I showered and dressed, slicking my hair back into a ponytail. I was on autopilot as I got into my car and drove over to Dr. Palmer's practice, where I found that falling back on routine and responsibility settled me some.

I met Dr. Rosa Palmer eight months ago, at a gathering for the creation of the pre-med sorority I had championed. She also had worked with Dr. Tim Rust, who was our town doctor, and knew him well, respected him immensely. Since Dr. Rust was expecting to turn his practice over to me, I wanted to live up to his expectations, as well as the expectations of this dynamic woman who was giving me a great deal of her time and energy to help me realize my goals.

When I made the decision to change from stats to premed, I contacted her and asked for her advice. She offered me the opportunity to shadow her at her internal medicine practice, beginning when I returned to school last fall. An opportunity I jumped at, because I was a year behind. But because I had already taken biology and chemistry, I was able to take the two dreaded o-chem classes right away. I'd eked out a solid A in the fall, but could barely keep my head above water this semester.

Once I reached the office I was, as usual, going non-stop, which helped, because then I didn't have time to obsess about what was bothering Booker.

About halfway into the morning, during a patient lull, I decided call him. Maybe he would be willing to talk to me. I knew he wouldn't change his mind about the wedding. I knew he loved me with everything in him. But I got a horrible, sick feeling at the very thought of losing him. It would crush me. But before I could get my phone out, Dr. Palmer poked her head out of her office and said, "Aubree, come on in."

When I walked in, she said, "Close the door and have

a seat." I felt my shoulders knot and my stomach clench.

"I usually hold my assessment of a med student in reserve until I get to know the person, observe that person in action, and see what potential is there. I have done the same thing with you, Aubree. But after having you shadow me these past eight months, I am happy to tell you what an absolute gem you are, and how thrilled I am to have you participating in my practice.

"Not only are you always on time, and take this volunteer position seriously, but my patients love you. Your bedside manner is endearing and warm, yet with just the right amount of professionalism."

"Thank you, Dr. Palmer."

"Because of your professionalism, your potential as a physician, and your brilliant mind, I would very much like to write a recommendation for you to med school."

"That would be fantastic. Thank you."

"In addition, I happened to see your article in the *Tulane Hullabaloo* on bedside manner. I found it touching, comical, and very enlightening. I have contacted the AMA, and they also would very much like you to be our keynote speaker to kick off the Student Research Symposium in June."

I bit my lip. "When in June?"

"The twenty-second."

"I would be honored, of course, but I'm getting married on the twentieth, and we're supposed to be on our honeymoon on the twenty-second, although we haven't worked out where we want to go yet."

"Congratulations, Aubree!"

"I didn't mention it because we haven't had a chance to discuss whether I would continue my shadowing during the summer."

"That's not a problem. Most med students do other programs and activities in the summer. I fully expected you would take the summer off and be back in the fall. At least I hope so. Now that we've discussed your future, why don't you tell me what's wrong."

"What do you mean?"

"I know a few things about you, Aubree. One of them is you're a perfectionist."

"It's that obvious?"

"I'm afraid so. I know all about it, because I'm one, too. You're classic. You cultivate your character, set improvement goals, don't flaunt your achievements, and when you get distracted, you get tougher on yourself, especially if you think you've made mistakes."

I couldn't answer her right away. Panic, fear, and helplessness overwhelmed me, and a huge lump gathered in my throat. I shifted and crossed my legs, gripping the handrests. Trying to sound normal, I made myself speak. "I'm sure you're very busy and don't have time—"

There was a hint of censure in her voice when she replied, "Let me be the judge of how I spend my time."

"I'm just tired, Dr. Palmer. That's all." I rose and smiled for emphasis. I was desperate to get out of her office before I made a fool of myself. I couldn't tell her what was wrong since I wasn't exactly sure.

There was a strained silence; then Dr. Palmer spoke again. "I see. I understand if you don't want to trust me with the particulars." The tone of her voice was so kind and gentle, and it reminded me of my momma. I felt the need to call Momma, but still struggled with the feeling that I should be able to handle this on my own.

Dr. Palmer continued, "I just want you to know that I hope you will feel free to ask me questions, ask for help you might need with your studies, with anything. Becoming a doctor is grueling. I know how hard it is, Aubree."

Tears burned my eyes, and I busied myself with

turning the knob so she wouldn't see. Swallowing hard, I said, "Thank you for everything. I'm sorry about the AMA."

I wasn't ready to admit my shortcomings to my mentor. Not willing to say out loud that maybe there was something wrong in my relationship, and it was probably all my fault. It had always been important to me to be on top of everything, and to admit I wasn't... well, I just couldn't.

I headed directly for the ladies' room, and when the door swung shut behind me, I buried my face in my hands. Shoot, I had made such a mess of things. And I didn't know what to do to put them right.

That hollow feeling never left me for an instant. I tried to slog through my classes, attend my sorority meeting, and, once I got back to our empty cottage in New Orleans' French Quarter, write another article for the *Hullabaloo*, but everything was rote.

When my phone rang, my insides knotted, and, with a rush of anticipation, I grabbed my phone.

"Hey there, Aubree." It was Ashley, my former roommate from Tulane. "How about a quick drink? You can bring the old ball and chain if you want to."

"Uh, Booker's busy, and I'm—"

"Don't you dare say you're swamped. So am I, but I'm making an effort to hang out with my best friend."

Sighing, I admitted it was true. I hadn't seen Ashley in forever, and hadn't made an effort to fix it. I struggled with guilt and shame over not contacting her, and said, "All right, but just an hour."

"Better than nothing. I'll meet you in fifteen at *Rupert's*. The last one there is a chicken."

After I hung up, I dropped down on the bed, my legs weak, my eyes scratchy from lack of sleep, and tried to call Booker, but it went to voice mail. I thought about him sitting in bed, the way the sheet had fallen away from his beautifully muscled chest, the way his biceps had bunched when he leaned forward, draping those strong arms across his knees. The welcome and warmth in his oh-so-blue eyes, the fall of his silky, shaggy black hair.

All he'd asked was to have dinner with me, but all my commitments were not only wearing on me, they were taking me away from him. I hadn't meant for him to feel that he wasn't a priority. If I'd hurt him... His expression, those slow, disappointment movements while he covered his glorious nakedness with that sexy jock, told me everything.

It hit me then and hit me now. He was everything.

For the first time since I got involved with him, I got a taste of what it would be like to have to live without him.

CHAPTER TWO

Boone

TRIPDAR was the word we used for the cosmic energy that seemed to swirl around multiple births. All three of us felt it, deep in the psyche, when one of us was stressed and unhappy.

I'd been having that sensation, and it was keeping me up at night. Verity was beginning to notice, and since she hadn't said anything about Aubree, it looked like my soon-to-be sister-in-law was not communicating with her friends.

I was currently working at the Eula Downs racetrack setting in the spring plantings. I wiped the sweat from my forehead and pushed send on my phone. "Booker is back," Brax and I said at exactly the same time.

"Something is up," Brax growled. Even though he was incredibly happy, he hadn't changed much. He was still a contrary SOB. "It's girl trouble."

"How do you know?"

"I get this ache at the base of my skull when women are involved. I got it when you were having your troubles with Verity, and the first time Booker and Aubree were figuring out their relationship. It feels familiar, and no amount of pain reliever makes it go away."

"I can't sleep."

"Well, let's go over there. I'm sure he's home. We can kick his ass, and then at least you and I will feel better."

"Ha! Right. We're meddling huckleberries."

#

Booker

I was sitting on the back porch staring off into the bayou, my phone beside me, but it was still turned off. I was being a jackass, but I didn't know what to say to Aubree right now. Maybe I wasn't strong enough for this.

The house was in great shape since my ma, or Boone, or Brax came by once a week to check on it. Pick up the junk mail and do any maintenance that was required. I couldn't even use picking up the house as an outlet.

I was so involved in feeling sorry for myself that I actually jumped when Brax materialized in front of me. He crouched down so he was eye to eye with me. "Hey, huckleberry. How long you been home?"

Boone was standing next to him. I should have known I couldn't hide out here for long. "Two days."

"And you didn't contact your brothers? That's rude, don't you think, Brax?"

"Totally."

I leaned back on my elbows and smirked at my brothers. It was hopeless. I couldn't stay in a funk when they were around. It was impossible. "What do you two jokers have up your sleeves? I can see it in your eyes."

"Oh, we thought you'd want the Gummy Bears we've been saving for you."

"You did?" I looked at Boone. "You promised me red ones."

"So I did." He leaned his arm on Brax's shoulder and danger signals went off at the look in their eyes. "You got some at your house, Brax?"

"Yeah, I do. With Booker's name on them."

"Right," I said. "Sure you do."

Boone's brows lifted. "You won't know until you come with us."

I snatched up my phone went down the steps with them. Anything would be better than sitting here feeling sorry for myself.

I got into Boone's truck and we took off.

"How's the writing going?" Brax asked.

"Pretty good. I'm about three quarters of the way through book five. I have been talking to a producer through email since November."

"No shit!"

"Yeah, these things can fall through, though. They just made me an offer for a movie deal for the first three books. I talked to an entertainment lawyer, and he's reviewing the contract. Of course this is for options, but it's amazing money, and it's on track to be made into movies. Gotta be the ultimate thing."

"Man, that's so cool," Boone said.

"Yeah," I agreed, but it would have been a lot cooler if I had been able to tell Aubree first, broken the news to her over dinner, then made love to her all night. Success was great, but it was even better shared with someone important. I smiled as my brothers talked about going to Hollywood for the premiere, and how I was about to become a household word.

I couldn't say I wouldn't enjoy the attention, the book signings, and the chance to interact with my readers. Unlike some authors, I was more of an extrovert. I had a pretty strong presence online, but had been to only one reader conference. But there was one coming up this summer I wanted to attend. I guess

Aubree and I would have to work out our schedules.

Thinking of Aubree again made me long for those days last summer when we were together every day, hanging out and enjoying ourselves. We'd been through quite a bit together, building our relationship through adversity and tremendous emotional turmoil. We'd believed we had a bright future together. Our relationship was still strong, but recently I was feeling unhappy.

I was making my point by giving her some distance. I had another reason, too, and it was embarrassing and lame, but I couldn't seem to get past it. I had felt vulnerable, open and exposed.

I knew she was tired, but I was still irritated...and I didn't want to be. It was more painful, pierced me more deeply than anything I'd experienced before. I guess I was having growing pains. I'd pretty much gone from high school into writing and had never been tied to a job or had limitations, which suited me down to the ground.

I hated limitations, but maybe I needed to change my assumptions. Maybe I needed to reassess how much I could handle, what was my breaking point.

Was I being too hard on Aubree? On myself?

It hurt to know that medicine may be a top priority in her life, maybe a more important priority than our relationship. The amount of time, effort and money that had to go into it was enormous. Although maybe becoming a doctor had to take priority right now. I just needed to feel she was also invested in our relationship. Losing her love wasn't an option. Damn near sent me into a tailspin to think that it was even possible.

"Booker!"

"What?"

"Geez, you *are* preoccupied. I asked if you wanted to come down to Outlaws tonight and sing with us."

"Oh, yeah, sure."

My brothers exchanged looks, and I was pretty surprised they weren't pumping me for information. Nosy bastards. But I guess they were nosy because I was keeping Boone up nights, and obviously Brax had been affected, too. We were trips, after all.

When we walked into Brax's house, River Pearl was in the kitchen. She smiled and gave me a hug and a kiss on the cheek. "Hello, stranger. How's Aubree?"

Even her name made my gut clench.

"Busy," I said, trying to keep my churning emotions out of the word, but it came out short and a bit harsh.

River's brows rose and her eyes narrowed. "I think I need to get in touch with her. She's been out of the loop for weeks. Did you know she still hasn't gotten a gown?"

Her words were like a bomb dropping on me, exploding and turning me into raw hamburger. My gut lurched and I went completely still. "What do you mean she hasn't gotten a gown? That's the first thing brides-to-be do, isn't it?"

I was like most guys when it came to weddings. I did my bit. Got the church locked down, bought the wedding rings, thought about the honeymoon, even though I hadn't committed to any plans yet. The fact that Aubree hadn't attended to this one important detail sent me into a tailspin of doubt. Was she having doubts?

"Sugar," Brax said, "why don't you do that?" He took her arm and drew her away from me, but the damage was already done. Brax talked to her in low tones, and I just stood there like I was paralyzed.

"Girls," Boone said, punching me in the arm. "Always so dramatic, right?"

"When did Verity buy her dress?"

Boone shuffled his feet and looked out the window over the sink. "Uh, she started making it the minute she had a chance, after the Billy Joe attack and our figuring everything out thing. It doesn't mean anything. Maybe Aubree isn't the typical...uh...girl."

I felt sick and leaned back against the doorframe. "No, she's completely typical. Getting married is a big deal, Boone. Why hasn't she gotten her dress?"

"There could be a lot of reasons why."

I could hear it in his voice. Maybe there were reasons, but why hadn't she mentioned it? My nerves jumped, giving me a warning tremor as the situation seemed to slip a little further out of my control.

River gave me a look and kissed Brax. "I'm heading out to the gallery. I'll be back later." She slipped past me and the front door closed softly.

Boone said cheerily, "Hey, let's play—"

"I'm not in the mood for video games," I said, struggling to hold on to my composure. My phone burned a hole in my pocket, but stubbornly I held off. I had vowed I wouldn't talk to her until I had worked some stuff out, and I was sticking to that until I was ready.

"You want to eat?"

"Not hungry."

"Let's spar, then."

My head came up and my eyes narrowed. "Spar? Is that why you brought me here? Drunk fighting?"

"Come on, Book. You're tense. You could loosen up."

"And spill my guts?"

"If guts get spilled, well, you know shit happens. Who are we to judge?" Brax said. "I've spilled my guts enough to you guys, and we're bros. We stick together no matter what."

I looked at Boone. "What the hell happened to him?"

"Five feet eleven inches of kick-ass bombshell."

"Did she cut off your balls?"

Brax smirked. "No, but she does seem to be real

24

interested in that area. What can I say?"

"And, he's baaaaack," I smirked, too, even through my misery.

"What do you have for us to go a few rounds?"

Boone smiled and Brax chuckled. "Your favorite. Sugar State Fruit Punch Moonshine."

"Gummy Bears, my ass," I snorted.

"It's red, like Gummy Bears," Brax said, walking over and pulling a jar out of the fridge. He grabbed three shot glasses and headed toward the room where he kept his boxing equipment.

I huffed a laugh, sighed, and followed. I wasn't as physical as my two brothers. I'd rather talk things out— unless, of course, Aubree was being threatened. Then all bets were off.

As I walked into the room, Brax set the glasses and the 'shine down on the mat. I pulled off my T-shirt. He grabbed up a couple of rolls of tape and chucked one at Boone and one at me. We caught them and I started to unroll it and wrap it around my fingers, my hand, and over my knuckles.

"You go first, Book. Take on Brax. I'll start drinking."

The rules of our drunk fighting game were simple. Whenever someone got hit, Boone would have to drink. Then we would rotate out. Brax was good, so hitting him was a challenge, but as he knew, I might not be as bulked out as my brothers, but I could be a dirty fighter.

And I was feeling in the mood for some tension release.

"Ladies and gentlemen," Boone bellowed. "This is drunk fighting, and the only rules are no hitting below the belt unless it's with your words. That's totally allowed." Brax thumbed his nose and grinned. "On my left we have Booker, who's a scrapper and a tricky devil, weighing in at one-seventy-nine. On my right we have Brax, who's fast and wily and weighs in at one-eighty-eight. And this moonshine that packs a punch, and is damn good, weighs in at thirty-two ounces."

"And, you weigh in at two hundred and five, and all of it is in your muscled head," Brax growled. I laughed and he looked at me, tilting his chin. "A hundred on the can," he said.

"What can?" I played along.

"The one where I'm the can and you're the ass, huckleberry. I'm bringing the whup."

"If we're talking about asses, here...well, I don't trade hee-haws with a jackass," I snarled. "I'll see you and raise you a hundred."

Boone burst out laughing and said, "Do you want your frilly apron, Brax? That'll show him who's boss."

Brax turned and gave an evil cackle, pointing his finger at Boone. "You're next, sweetheart," he said. "I'll show you pink...and some black and blue."

"Looking forward to it," Boone said, narrowing his eyes, but it was ruined by their lurking twinkle.

We danced around each other, warming up. Brax's blue eyes were full of mischief and determination. It was like looking into my own face; even our body types were so similar it was eerie. Made us almost evenly matched. Boone had more muscle, so more power, but that was it.

"Start!"

Brax took my left on his shoulder, but I was expecting his weaving move, he was so slick, that when he dodged, I was ready with my right and socked him right on the jaw. That rocked him back. He tongued his lip, lapping up the blood and smiled.

"Nice, Book. Good cheap shot."

Boone downed a shot glass.

I grinned. "Kiss my can."

Brax hadn't changed a helluva lot. He still was an angry sumbitch. He swung a powerful right at me, which I blocked, but then his left landed in my midriff. I retaliated with a left to the body and a right to the side of the head. Brax immediately followed with an uppercut. He was so damn fast, and the two blows hardly fazed him.

His fist connected with my chin and rattled my teeth, the blow jarring and exploding up through muscle and bone.

Getting hit with taped knuckles was pretty different from getting hit with gloves, less stunning, but it still hurt. We were pulling our punches, obviously, but still. Brax could hit and hit hard when he wanted to.

I stumbled back and landed on my butt on the mat. "Drink time," Boone bellowed. Brax offered me help up. I clasped his hand and he pulled. We were grinning like idiots.

We bumped fists, and I slapped Boone's open hand as he passed me. "Go get 'im, tiger."

Boone swaggered out there, and Brax and he circled around each other. Brax was definitely faster than Boone, but Boone was a tank. He took gut punches like he was waving off mosquitoes.

"Izzat all you have? Geez, Brax, Verity can hit harder than that."

Brax growled and charged him, and they hit the mat in a tumble of arms and legs. I was busy downing shots each time one of them landed a face or head blow.

Laughing like a fool, I could tell Boone was feeling the effects of the moonshine, but I would never discount my brother. Boone had so much heart.

They got up at the same time, neither the worse for wear. Boone took a left on his shoulder and hooked a left to Brax's body, and Brax grunted when it connected. Boone followed with a straight to the mouth and a left hook to the side of the head. They clinched, and Boone clubbed Brax with a right to the ribs.

The moonshine shots went down easy, the fruit punch taste lingering on my tongue.

"Break it up," I said, my gut feeling warm and the alcohol loosening the tension in my shoulders.

They broke apart and Brax retreated. "Not bad, Boonie."

Boone grinned hugely, and I stood up as Brax plopped down and stretched out to reach for a towel. Wiping off the sweat, he gave Boone a knowing look.

"So, Book, you want to tell us what the hell is going on with you and Aubree?"

"I'm not nearly drunk enough to talk about girls, let alone about Aubree."

Boone gave Brax a *nice try* look.

"We care about Breebree. There's trouble in paradise and we want to know—"

I gave him a thunderous look. "Are we going to spar or jabber like squealing schoolgirls?"

I was feeling a bit wobbly, and since I was the lightest of the three of us, I was feeling the effects of the 100-proof hooch.

Boone looked up at me, still breathing hard. "You going to fight or be a candy ass?"

I said, "Can't believe I've got to deal with two Dr. Phils."

Boone giggled at that and pushed up from the floor with the kind of power that came with all that muscle. He started with a left swing to my head, and during the ensuing wild mix-up he landed four right and left hooks right on my ribs. I grunted and tried to backheel him, but failed, and he lowered his head and butted me in the belly, kicked me on the shin, and would have banged me up some more, but the alcohol was surging, and I was riding an adrenaline high. I stopped him in his tracks by swinging an overhand right to the back of his neck, which took the fight out of him for a minute.

We clinched, and I learned that my brother was part octopus. We grappled some more, then Brax, after downing several shots, got up and broke us up.

Boone went for the moonshine, and I faced Brax.

"You're not going to make me beat the information out of you? Are you?"

"You guys think you're both so s-smart." The alcohol was starting to go to my head with the exertion. I took a breath, swore, then swore again.

"Come on," he said, after a couple more long moments. "There's a Boy Scout badge in it for you," Brax promised, not quite managing a grin. He was goading me. Probably thought it was for my own good, and he might be right. But he also couldn't be all that amused. He knew how much it hurt to be on the outs when passionately in love.

"Screw—"

"Me. Yeah. I got it," he said under his breath, giving Boone a long-suffering sigh.

Then it got real. Brax, even under the influence, was dangerous. He swung a right to my body, and while I didn't think I landed a solid punch to his ribs, he staggered and dropped his hands slightly.

I straightened out of my defensive crouch and cocked my right, and realized I had been suckered.

The minute I lifted my chin, he beat me to the punch with a right that smashed my head back until I saw some serious stars. Dazed and only partly conscious of what was going on, I rebounded right into him, ramming my jaw flush into his left hook. Ka-*bam*! At the same instant I hooked a trip-hammer right under his heart, and we hit the floor together.

I could hear yelling and cursing, but wasn't sure it was me or him, and I felt like my head was bouncing around in a thick fog. All I knew was I had to get back on my feet as fast as I could. Brax wouldn't cut me any quarter. I was reeling when I rose, my legs barely holding me. Brax was ready, and I saw the light of the battle in his eyes, and saw my winning move. I rushed in wide open, staking everything on one right swing.

I stepped inside his fight-finishing swing, and went for the one-two punch, sinking my fist into his gut, and quickly, with the same hand hammered up under his jaw. He staggered, his arms fell, and I swung my left with my full body weight behind it. Brax hit the floor and Boone surged to his feet.

"Geezus, Booker!"

Breathing hard, I looked down at Brax, who was looking up at me, his eye swelling even as I watched.

"What the hell is going on in here!?" River Pearl's voice cut across all of us like ice against the skin.

Brax's head lifted and his eyes widened. "Oh, sheee-it," it came out slurred and urgent.

I felt like I was disassembling...breaking up into tiny pieces... couldn't hold myself together. Needed Aubree. Needed to talk to her, but the room whirled and dipped.

"We're not mad at each other," Boone slurred. "It's just drunk fighting. We're trying to get Booker to..." he hiccupped, "...talk."

"Oh my God. You're drunk? God save me from brothers."

Boone giggled and said, "Hey, that's what Breebree says."

She slapped her palm against her face and groaned. "One is enough to deal with, but three..." She groaned again. "Well you're done."

Brax was on his feet. "No we're not," Boone said. "Not until one of us pukes or passes out.

Brax punched him in the gut and Boone heaved.

I closed my eyes, dropped to my knees, then collapsed face-first onto the mat.

I dimly heard Brax say, "Now we're done," before my brain shut down.

CHAPTER THREE

Aubree

I CHECKED my phone after class and my heart sank. Still no calls from Booker, going on two days now.

I was hurrying to my car when a horn blasted right in my ear. I stopped dead, my head whipping around to see an angry driver yelling out his window, waving his fist. "Watch where you're going! I almost hit you! I have a daughter your age, for God's sake."

He waited, his face pinched, probably from fear, his hand tapping on the wheel.

"I'm sorry."

"Next time be more careful."

"I will."

With a curt nod, he drove off.

My heart pounding, I sat in my car for a minute, squeezing my eyes shut, and taking a deep breath. I had no time for wallowing, because I was almost late for my hours at Dr. Palmer's office. Even though Dr. Palmer was always very understanding, I found it very upsetting to be late.

Fortunately I found a parking spot close to her practice, and ran the last few feet, and arrived only five minutes ahead of my assigned hours.

As I stored my things, I fretted about what was going on with Booker. Since the stupid *man* hadn't told me what was wrong, I had no way to know what he was upset about, how he was feeling.

I was painfully aware now of how badly I had dropped the ball with regard to my personal life. My life with him. But when I started having so much trouble mastering o-chem, I lost track of just about everything.

I grabbed a lab coat and went to work. Thankfully her practice was always busy, and the afternoon went by very fast. At closing time, my phone beeped and I pulled it out of my pocket.

What is going on? We're worried about you. Call me, or else.

Despite my disappointment that it wasn't Booker, and even though I was incredibly stressed out, I chuckled. "River Pearl," I said softly. She was such a good friend, and I knew putting her off wasn't going to work.

But even now I couldn't bring myself to talk to one of my best friends.

I covered my face and leaned against the wall, swamped by a tidal wave of shame over all the ways I was screwing up. I was failing at everything. I burst into tears, and when I felt hands on my shoulders steering me, I just let the person move me along.

I was led to a seat and gently pushed down into it. Heard a door close.

When I looked up, Dr. Palmer was leaning against her desk. She always looked so put together, with her hair pulled up, her flawless makeup, her stylish clothes.

She just stood there studying me with a small frown. "Would it help to talk about it?"

I swallowed and looked out the window, stalling. People were walking by like everything was normal, and here I was going under for the third time.

A Perfect Wedding

It had been almost three days since Booker left, almost three days of nearly unbearable silence, two nights when I missed his warm, comforting presence in our bed. Now I was losing it in front of a woman who could make or break me in medicine.

"I'm just—"

"Tired? I'm not buying it," Dr. Palmer pressed. "I've seen a change in you this spring. And you're miserable, even though you're doing your best not to show it."

Dr. Palmer leaned forward intently. She gave me a warm, compassionate look and said quietly, "I know what's it's like to be in your shoes. I remember the exhaustion, the juggling, the doubts, and the fear of failure. For me it was all about my dad and living up to his expectations. So don't try to snow me. I've been there."

Quickly wiping my eyes with the side of my hand, I tried to answer her, but I was so full of fear and misery I couldn't speak.

Her expression lit with warm concern, she leaned closer and looked me in the eyes. "No matter how scared and alone you feel, you're not."

I wiped my eyes again and let out a shaky sigh. I wasn't alone. I had Booker. I knew he wasn't going to abandon me. He wouldn't. Not after all we'd been through. But I was worried about him.

Dr. Palmer leaned back, pulled a tissue out of the box on her desk, and offered it to me.

I took it and thanked her while I mopped up my tears.

"So tell me, Aubree. What is wrong?"

I closed my eyes and everything poured out in a rush...how I was trying to juggle my classes and was failing miserably in o-chem, how I was feeling ineffectual, and finally how I had fallen asleep on Booker, and worse, how I had neglected him. And how he'd left after I fell asleep and now wasn't answering his phone or responding to my texts.

"Ah, you're scared you're going to lose him."

"No. Booker wouldn't leave me. But I am concerned about what he's going through. Nothing makes sense without him, not even being a doctor."

"Aubree, I have to be honest with you. I had a rocky road with the man who is now and has been my husband for eighteen years. Our relationship was much like yours, but he made a decision to stand by me no matter what happened. There were times when I scarcely saw him, because if you think it's hard now... honey, it's only begun. Next year you will have to study for your Medical College Admission Test, the dreaded MCAT, then there's applications and interviews, then med school, and residency. Becoming a doctor is grueling, hard on you, and even harder on those you love.

"So it's better now to know, before you commit to marriage, whether he's going to be your rock-solid supporter or a hindrance. On the other hand, it's just as important to have balance in your life. Choose what's important and don't worry about the rest. Medical schools are looking for a well-rounded student, not a perfect one."

"Booker would never be a hindrance. He's so good to me. So, is this a pep talk?" I said. "I'm afraid it's not a very good one."

"The truth actually does set you free, but sometimes it's tough to take."

"I want to be a doctor. It's my dream. But I won't sacrifice Booker."

"Do you trust him?"

"With my life." I might have gotten sidetracked by my own bullshit, but I knew—had always known—one thing for certain. Booker would never let me down. He was struggling, and he might be pissed or teaching me a lesson, but he would never, ever abandon me. The proof of that was written in the Langstons' blood

"You didn't hesitate. That's good. The bottom line, then, is to work it out with Booker. Come to an understanding you both can live with."

I leaned back. Here was maturity and wisdom staring me in the face. I wanted to be with Booker, and was confused and overwhelmed about how to get what I wanted *and* what he wanted.

Worse, we hadn't discussed any of this. We hadn't realized, I think, how hard it would be. A relationship was built on every day, and grew out of every choice each person made.

With a sharp pang in my heart, I admitted to myself that I had taken him for granted. I had fallen down on that task. Lost myself to my need to excel. Something I believed I had conquered, but obviously had not. And it was going to be a battle, and require constant vigilance for me—for us—to overcome.

"Now, let's talk about organic chemistry."

I groaned. That stupid subject was ruling my life. I wanted to get away, go home, but I didn't want to face the empty rooms. Without Booker it had ceased being home. But I had no choice. I had a paper to write, and more o-chem homework, and I absolutely had to master the subject before I flunked the damn class. And have no chance at medical school.

What I wanted to do was to get in my car and drive to Suttontowne. To Booker. To apologize to him, and just hang on to him. But I wasn't sure he'd let me do that right now.

The memory from Old Magnolia Road blindsided me. He barely knew me back then, but while Damien's blood seeped into the road and his dead eyes stared up at us, Booker had pulled me against him. Kissed my temple, held me tight. The terrible fear inside me for him, for his safety hadn't let me just collapse.

Dear God, I had thought fervently, *don't let him be hurt*. I checked him over thoroughly, running my hands over his chest and body to make sure there were no knife wounds, no injuries. That's when he'd grabbed my hands, pulled them to his chest and quieted me. And then he helped me bury Damien.

Even now I couldn't feel remorse for what had happened.

Back then I chose to abandon him and run. Just like I had done when I witnessed his breakdown at the bleachers. I chose then to chalk up our encounter to the adrenaline and the horror of what we had done.

I had been a coward then, but I had matured a bit, and I had fallen so deeply into him, there was no way out.

Even as Dr. Palmer laid out how she would help me with o-chem, how it could be managed, understood and conquered. I was thinking how my life was so entwined with Booker's, I couldn't believe we had managed to create this silent void between us.

As I walked to my car, a rush of feelings for him overwhelmed me, and I knew, simply, that Booker needed me. Much more now than ever. And it appeared I had some more maturing to do.

I hoped he knew in his heart I would never abandon him again. I hoped that what I believed were strength and harmony and undying commitment between us wasn't misplaced.

Because losing him would cost me something much too precious and fundamental. My heart. He was my heart. I wasn't sure I could survive that loss.

#

A Perfect Wedding

Braxton

Before River Pearl, I might have kept my thoughts about Aubree and Booker's turmoil to myself. Hurt for him, but kept my own counsel. Before River Pearl, I might have thought Aubree and Booker were doomed to fail. Before her, I lived in a wasteland.

But that all changed with her love, with her acceptance, and the way she had fought for me, for my family. The way she had changed everything.

"What the hell were you thinking, Braxton Michael Outlaw!"

Uh-oh, she was using my middle name, and she was in a Southern snit like I'd never seen.

"Is this any way to treat your brother when you know he's upset, angry, and lost? Beating each other up is *crazy*...you and Boone should have your *heads* examined."

"Hey, we meant well," Boone said, looking green around the gills because we were still pretty drunk.

Booker had gone out like a light, the lightweight huckleberry. Part of that was stress, the other was not sleeping, and some of it could have been the quantity of Fruit Punch Red he'd consumed. He was currently sleeping it off in our guest room while River scolded and whipped us into shape.

"Take a breath, sugar," I said. She whirled on me and crowded me up against the wall, her eyes blazing.

"Don't you dare make light of this. I care about Aubree and Booker! We have to do something to help them."

I reached up and clasped her arms as Boone sidled toward the door, looking spooked. He should. If River were to call Verity, his ass would be in a sling, right along with mine.

I leaned slightly around River. "Freeze, huckleberry."

He sighed and leaned against the wall. It was clear the alcohol buzz was clearing and he was starting to feel the cuts and contusions.

"Maybe we should get Verity over here for a powwow?" Boone said.

"Well, aren't you the freaking hero?" I said, knowing that next on the agenda would be some haranguing from one hopped-up preacher's daughter. "The alcohol must have gone to your brain."

"I called Verity and she's on her way."

Boone groaned and slid down the wall.

"I see that the usual shenanigans have ensued when the three wildest men in Suttontowne get together. It's almost like you can't help yourselves," Verity said from the doorway and Boone moaned again.

"Where's Booker?" Verity said.

"He's in oblivion, which is where I wish I was right now."

Verity crouched down. "Ah, sugar, I never hit a man when he's down. So as soon as you're back on your feet..."

Boone chuckled. "It was Brax's idea," he said, a crazy grin on his face as he reached up and cupped his wife's face. She shook her head and covered his hand. "I'm sure it was your idea, actually, but I said for better or for worse."

"That's right," he said with the same goofy grin. "So you're stuck."

I laughed. We sure picked ourselves some fine women. I shook my head and looked back at River Pearl. Yup, that sassy sugar wasn't done. As she wound up to cuss me out again, I planted my lips over hers. She protested for all of three seconds, her words muffled against my mouth, and then she sighed and kissed me back.

I cupped her face and ended the kiss. "River. We've

been doing this drinking game for a long time. It helps us blow off steam and get this shit out of our heads and out in the open so we can talk about it. That's all we were trying to do with Booker. It got a little out of hand."

She bit her lip, but some of the pique left her eyes. "A little," she huffed and rubbed her thumb gently along my jaw. "You're going to have a black eye."

"Will you kiss it better for me if I beg you?" I whispered in her ear and the hand that went around my nape clutched tight in my hair as she sighed again.

"It's going to have to be later." She kissed me again, then said, "Verity, are you packed and ready to go?"

"Yes. I left our handsome little devil Duel with Ethan, since I thought you were at work, Boone. You can pick him up after you get sober."

"Where are you two going?" I asked.

River Pearl got that juggernaut look in her eye. The kind of look that meant she was about to drop-kick Aubree into gear. I almost felt sorry for Aubree, but it was all about how much River cared and I knew whatever was good for Aubree is what River was all about. "We're going to New Orleans. It's time Aubree got serious about this wedding. We should never have allowed her to put us off this long. As maid of honor, I'm going to wrassle that girl to the mat and make her do some planning. You stay here and—"

"Help my stupid brother."

"And..." she said, her eyes narrowing.

"No more drunk fighting. We'll just take him into the swamp and stake him out until the mosquitoes make him talk."

"All right," she said, "But absolutely no wrestling gators."

"Aww, sugar, you are no fun."

She grabbed my chin. "Seriously, Brax, take care of him."

"That's always my priority, *ma belle.*"

Booker

I knew three things when I woke up: one, I fucking missed Aubree; two, I was crazy sick in love with her; and three, I ached all over like a son of a bitch. Dammit. Why did I ever let my stupid brothers talk me into drunk fighting? I should have heeded Aubree's warning when I promised her I wouldn't let my brothers talk me into something stupid. My mouth hurt, my jaw hurt, my gut hurt, and my brain was rolling around in my head like a big, hard, dumb-ass marble.

But mostly my heart hurt...bad. How many times would I screw up with this girl?

Disoriented, I shifted and realized I was on a bed. I had the mother of all headaches. I opened my eyes... well, one of them. The other one was swollen and only gave me a slit's worth of information.

I was in Brax's spare room. I recognized the pattern on the curtain and the view from the window.

I rolled toward the door and groaned.

Something cold pressed against my eye, and I looked up to see my worse-for-wear brothers standing there. I felt better and sighed at the relief. I wasn't the only one with a black eye.

Boone handed me some pain reliever and a glass of water after I sat up and scooted back. They sat down. "Heads up. Verity and River Pearl are on their way to The Big Easy for a wedding planning intervention."

I took the pills and chased them with some water. "She needs some help. I still can't believe she hasn't gotten her dress."

"At least the cake is covered," Brax said. "I've been practicing for weeks. Martha is doing the taste testing. She says she'll let me know when I get there. I talked to Aubree about her choices, but she doesn't want me to tell you. Wants it to be a surprise."

"I'm sure it will be great. Thanks for doing that, Brax. I know how busy you are."

"Never too busy for you and..." he shoved Boone, "... this huckleberry."

Boone shoved him back. "Feeling is mutual you jerkwad."

Brax smirked, then turned to look at me, sobering. It was completely weird to see my brother so...open, and different. River was a miracle worker.

"Book, you know we're here for you, but we can't give you any dumb-ass, sage, or unwanted advice until you tell us what's going on," Brax said.

"What's going on? Nothing. Aubree's been so...busy... that I haven't seen her. Whenever I try to get some time with her, she's *busy*!" I shouted and it echoed in the room. I lowered my voice. "I guess I'm pissed off."

"You having second thoughts?"

"No, dammit. Never. It's just that I acted like a jerk. I shouldn't have come back here without talking to her, but I was so annoyed. I didn't want to say something I couldn't take back. Now I'm calmer, I know I should have talked to her sooner instead of always swallowing it. My fault for not speaking up, but she's studying so hard and working so hard, so I held off so I wouldn't upset or distract her."

"But now it's hard on you."

"What else?" Brax said with that knowing look.

"Ever since you fell in love with River Pearl, you're sharing way too much," I said and nudged him.

He chuckled. "She has some influence over me. Now spill your guts or I'll give you another freaking black eye."

"What do you want me to say?"

"That you're trying to do what you always do, Book. Avoid pain."

"I'm not..."

"Yes, you are. You're feeling all kinds of exposed. It's

hard to talk to them when we feel weak. But, Book, that's the best time to talk to them."

"He's right," Boone said. "When I feel the worst is when I need Verity the most. She's always been there for me. Through everything. So why don't you give Aubree the benefit of the doubt, stop avoiding her, and talk this shit out? You're getting married in a month, ferchrissake. She's finished with classes in three weeks. Tough it out, and then get down to serious discussions about your future. Set the ground rules now you know what you're in for."

I leaned my head back against the headboard. I hadn't told them I was scared she didn't need me. That she was coming into her own and there was no place for me. I couldn't tell them that, because it might make it real, and it made me look weak.

I nodded. "Thanks for..."

"Knocking some sense into you," Boone said.

Brax pushed him off the bed, and even though we were all in pain, we wrestled some more because we were just plain idiots and we all knew it.

Unbidden, I was blindsided by the memory of the night Langston bushwhacked me with that baseball bat and I woke up on Old Magnolia Road lying in Aubree's arms with Daniel Langston looming over us with a gun. I had known he wanted to hurt her then and had fought like a madman to save her. I told her to run, but she didn't. She had been all that mattered to me as I fought Langston in spite of a bad concussion. No matter how I looked at it, Aubree was my future, my life.

That girl *still* got to me.

She always would.

"Get the hell outta here so I can call my girl."

They nodded, stood, and grinned at me.

After they vacated the room, I pulled out my phone and winced when I saw how many of her calls and texts

I'd ignored.

I hit send. I wasn't sure she would be able to answer, because she was just finishing at Dr. Palmer's.

But she answered and said, "Oh, God, Booker."

"Yeah, it's me. The dumb-ass." I loved her. That had never changed, not from the first moment I'd seen her, but, geezus, I hadn't, ever, not from the very beginning, been able to figure out what to do with her. She was amazing, and I was a guy with a horrible rep, the worst possible choice, but it hadn't mattered to her. She reinforced that with her next words.

"You're not dumb," she said softly, and her voice added a smile to the words. "I *have* been preoccupied and I *have* been zoned out for months."

Now I heard the regret, and that tightened my gut, and I immediately opened my mouth to gloss over it and retreat. But that had gotten me into trouble with her in the first place. Even though it felt uncomfortable, I closed my eyes and said, "You've been trying to keep everything together, Aubree. I know that, but I need something more."

She drew a deep, uneven breath, her voice wobbling now. "As in, more than me?"

"Fuck no!" I said fiercely, kicking myself for not being clear. Some communicator I was. "That's not what I meant. I need more between us, sugar. That's all. I'm as committed to you now as I have ever been." I ached to hold her, comfort her, show her I wanted to be everything to her. "You are everything to me. So I need a closer relationship, and I want you physically. I want to be inside you, giving you pleasure, feeling that close to you. Damn, but I *want* you." My voice came out hoarse and sounding desperate.

She breathed a sigh. "Okay, that sounds good to me. I *want* you, too. Just the same way, and just as badly."

I breathed a little easier, not sure when my chest had

gotten so tight. "Good. I love you so much, Aubree. I'm sorry if I hurt you. I didn't mean to. I just was so tired of —"

"Me failing you."

"You didn't fail me. You never do that. Neglected me is more what I was thinking."

I heard our doorbell ring and Aubree swore. I'd never heard her swear like that.

"Someone is at the door."

"Go answer it. I'm pretty sure you'll be happy."

"Aren't you coming back to New Orleans?"

There it was. The question I was dreading. My next words stuck in my throat, and when I pushed them out, it was one of the hardest things I'd ever had to do, my gut clenching, a kernel of anxiety trying to develop into something more.

I wanted her semester to be over first. I wanted her to do what she had to do, but wanted more than that, too. Much more. I wanted time alone with her, uninterrupted time. We urgently needed a chance to talk, to sort things out. "I was thinking I should...stay here and give you the time you need to finish everything. I'll work on getting some of my wedding duties out of the way and up-to-date so you don't have to worry about them."

"Distance isn't going to make our issues go away."

She might have acknowledged that we needed each other as strongly as we ever did, but I wasn't going to kid myself that she wasn't still harboring doubts. And the only way we were ever going to put those doubts behind us was to have time to explore our feelings, to talk about all the things we had stored away over the past eight months. I knew in my heart that before we could move forward, we had to go back. And that was totally scary.

All those fears of abandonment came back at me. But

I breathed through them. My daddy hadn't left us. I reminded myself over and over. River Pearl had uncovered the shocking truth. Our daddy had been murdered by River Pearl's cousin, Earl. She had also proven that our ancestor, Duel Outlaw, had been an upstanding citizen, and that her lauded ancestor Colonel Beauregard Sutton was the one who caused Duel's hanging when he robbed a Confederate gold shipment while riding my ancestor's borrowed mare.

Our curse had been lifted, and all of us were so grateful to River for that. Now she and Verity were at the door, and they were going to be there for Aubree. We trips truly had found ourselves some stellar women.

"No, and we'll discuss every one of those issues as soon as you can focus on our personal relationship one hundred percent. Right now..." The doorbell rang again. "...focus on your studies and your job. Three weeks isn't that long."

She huffed softly, and I groaned. "Ah, who the hell am I kidding? It's going to feel like a freaking eternity. I'm going to miss you like hell. Call me when you can."

"Booker..." The doorbell sounded again and she made this soft sound in her throat. "We'll work this out." She sounded so distraught, and I hated it. "Oh, Booker, could you do me a huge favor?"

"Of course, my beautiful."

Her tone got lighter. "Dr. Rust was just named national Country Doctor of the Year. The town is even putting up a billboard for him, and there's going to be a celebration. Can you go for me and wish him well? Tell him I'm so sorry that I couldn't...make it. It's next weekend and I'm just so swamped...Oh dammit," she said when the knocking started. "Coming," she yelled, then she was back. "Get him something nice. I've got to go. I love you."

"Love you, too. Bye."

So *great*. We talked. I'd finally gotten it all straight in my head. I needed to back off. Except there was one little problem with my noble, self-sacrificing plan: It fucking sucked.

Yes, I'd screwed up, but she was mine. I wasn't giving her up without a fight, and if the damned doorbell hadn't rung, I would have told her that totally, hewn-in-stone, irrefutable goddamned fact.

CHAPTER FOUR

Aubree

I WAS nearly sick with relief after Booker and I finished our conversation. Nothing had been settled, and I knew we had some major issues to work out, but he was as committed now as he was before. I could hear it in his voice.

Another wave of relief swept through me, along with major irritation.

Who the hell was banging on my door? I gasped when I saw two familiar faces staring back at me through the glass of the double panel, four-paned front French doors. With a cry of joy, I opened the door and threw myself into Momma's arms. Booker's momma, Evie, stood next to her, and as soon as I finished hugging my momma, I gave her a tight one too.

"Well, if the girl won't come to Suttontowne, we'll bring Suttontowne to her."

My eyes popped open and I squealed with delight when I saw River Pearl and Verity coming up the walk.

I ran to them and hugged them just as hard. It was like a shot in the arm for them to show up out of the blue, just when I needed them the most.

"Come on in."

47

All of them had been to our place before, but even so they exclaimed again over its wonderful location, nestled in the Veux Carré, or the French Quarter, in one of the best cities in the world. I loved New Orleans with a passion, even its rowdiness, which I thought was quaint. Booker was the one who had discovered this three-story cottage, which was tucked away and completely hidden from the street.

We lived about five miles from Tulane, and less than a mile from Bourbon Street. Historically it had served as a servant's quarter condo, but after renovations—including a spacious, thirteen hundred square feet of wood floors, a lively street scene-patterned wallpaper in the kitchen creating a beautiful contrast with the stainless steel appliances, and a cozy living room with overstuffed brown and turquoise couch and chairs—it was a very comfortable living space. Booker liked to say we had enough throw pillows to cushion every back in New Orleans. Booker and I shared the top loft-like bedroom with a view of the French Quarter.

After all the hugging and greetings were exchanged, I said breathlessly, "What are you all doing here?"

River narrowed her eyes at me, and Verity gave me that look that said I should darn well know why they were there.

My momma said, "Well, sweetheart. Your soon-to-be momma-in-law and I had no idea your two friends were coming, or we would have coordinated better. But I suspect they're here for the very same reason we are."

"The wedding."

"Yeah," River said, rolling her eyes. "Just a minor, little ol' thang." Taking my arm, she led me to the sofa.

"I have lemonade in the fridge," I said, ready to get up.

But Evie pushed down on my head gently and said, "I'll get some for us, sugar."

A Perfect Wedding

She went into the kitchen and threw comments into the discussion while she got out the pitcher and five glasses, grabbed one of my pretty trays she had found on one of her scavenging forays and settled everything on it. She came back into the living room and poured and passed around glasses.

"Your wedding is a month away, and we've barely finalized the details. We're here to take over whatever you need us to do."

"About your gown..." River said.

Those words triggered immediate turmoil. I had put off getting my wedding dress. I didn't know why. It wasn't that I didn't want to marry Booker. It wasn't that I had doubts about us...well, at least about us getting married. My doubts were my own feeling of inadequacy when it came to juggling everything. It probably was just sheer exhaustion because of everything I'd been dealing with in the last eight months...or was some other kind of fear lurking in my subconscious, ready to leap out and bite me?

River looked at Verity, and she nodded. "We have a marvelous solution for that problem. Verity?"

I turned to my pretty friend Verity, loving the way her dark hair was untamed and wild. She'd gotten some layers trimmed into in the long black tresses, which framed her beautiful, glowing face. Her makeup, subtle shades of gray and purple, was lovely on her, her dark brown eyes highlighted by the dark liner.

She smiled and took my hands. "I know you said you didn't want a fuss. I know you said you didn't want us to go to a lot of bother. And I know you said you would find something when the time was right." I eyed the garment bag she had thrown over the back of the couch. "But..." she bit her lip and gave me a sheepish grin, "...I couldn't help myself."

"She designed you a dress!" River burst out, and then

gave an unapologetic smile when Verity raised her eyebrows at her.

"And, we helped, so all you need to do is try it on to make sure it fits properly," my momma said.

"It's so you, and breathtakingly beautiful," Evie said. "I can't believe little Verity Fairchild conjured it up out of her talented imagination."

"Thank you, Ma," Verity said, and then turned back to me. "I've been working on this dress since Booker proposed to you in the bayou when we were frogging."

"That's my son, so romantic," Evie said with a chuckle.

"It *was* romantic," I said, laughing. Exactly the kind of thing only an Outlaw would do. They were never conventional. "And Booker is the best thing that ever happened to me."

Evie reached over and squeezed my hand. "I think he would say the same thing about you." She looked over at my momma. "So, Aubree. We're also here because we noticed Booker's back in Suttontowne without you. We...uh....came to—"

"Meddle," River Pearl said. "So what gives?"

"I'm just so busy. Every minute. Booker was feeling... neglected, and he had a right to his feelings."

"Well," Evie said. "Booker can sometimes have tunnel vision when he wants something. Have you two been communicating?"

"No, not really. We've been...I've been... preoccupied."

"He'd better get used to it, because in this case...it might be a bit tougher than, well...brain surgery," Verity said, and they all laughed. "You're studying to become a doctor. That's huge and time-consuming."

"It's a learning curve," my momma said. "Every couple has to work that kind of thing out."

I nodded. Hoped they were right.

"Let's see the dress," I said to Verity, who took a deep breath and stood up.

"River, could you help me? Since you're taller, you can hold it up so she can get the full impact." She looked at me. "Okay, cover your eyes, and no peeking."

I did as she asked, impatient with curiosity and anticipation. This was actually happening! I was getting married to Booker.

I heard the zipper and a rustle of cloth. "Okay, open your eyes."

River was holding the dress up over her head so the hem cleared the floor. I studied it for what seemed like a long time, and then sighed softly.

Then I stood up, covered my face, then threw my arms out and whooped. "Wow! Verity...I don't know what to say. It's so beautiful and so perfect." And it was. A-line to fit nicely to my small waist and wider hips. And clean lines, since flouncy, fluffy clothes didn't suit me.

"It's Crystal Tulle embellished with lace motifs over a fitted satin skirt. I went for dramatic and sexy," Verity said.

The embroidery and beading were so unique, with swamp flowers expertly sewn in a wrapping, flawless spiral all the way from the bodice down to and around the train. There were trumpet and water lilies, along with ferns, curlicues, and embellishments. "Oh, Verity, the swamp flowers are the perfect touch. And so beautifully done."

"Those were Minnie's idea, so I can't take credit. She helped me some with the design. She is so amazing."

"Let me see the back," I said and River turned the dress. "Oh, my, definitely more than a little sexy, too."

Verity nodded. "Yep, gotta have that for Booker, and that was my idea."

"Right," River said. "He'll have fun unlacing you out

of that corset closure, too."

I blushed, and there was no hiding it on my white skin. River giggled. I hugged Verity, hard. "Bless you for ignoring every word I said."

She hugged me back just as hard.

After I released her, she reached down and pulled a USB drive out of her purse and offered it to me. "Here is a video of me making the dress, and all of us pitching in on the sewing. Boone recorded it for me, so you'll have to put up with his lame-assed comments."

Tears flooded my eyes as my throat tightened. I took the USB drive out of her hand, eager to watch it and add to my fond memories, to be watched and re-watched again later. After brushing away my tears, my momma hugged me too, and then we had another hug fest.

"Tomorrow we're going shopping." River held up her hand when I opened my mouth. "It's Saturday, and you have no classes, so we're going to have a day of fun, no protests," she admonished. I had no recourse but to smile and give in.

"We'll find the perfect veil, shoes and unmentionables," Evie said.

"Yes," River agreed, "...more fun for Booker."

"Of course, this has to be a perfect wedding!" Verity said.

"You all are the best. Thank you so much for doing this," I said, my voice shaky.

At midnight, even though I was bone tired, I couldn't settle after all the discussion and excitement with my friends and the mommas. I gave up my room to my momma and Evie. Verity and River got my guest room, and I opted for the comfortable pull-out couch. Hours after everyone else had bedded down, I went out to the courtyard and settled on a bench, resting against the wall behind me.

My mind wandered, anxiety eating at me, the dark of

night weighted by the hint of sultry heat on its way. I wondered if Booker could sleep, and ached to call him, but if he was sleeping, I didn't want to wake him. The weeks until I saw him again did feel like an eternity. I'd believed I had control of everything, including my constant need to excel, and my terrible perfectionism. But I had been wrong. My grueling schedule had brought it all back, pieces of the past resurrected. Maybe those traits were too ingrained in me.

The door opened and River came out to join me. Her long brown hair fluttered around her slim shoulders, playing against her slender ribs all the way to her waist.

She was wearing a white tank top and a pair of barely-there yoga shorts, her feet bare. She was carrying two glasses, and—bless her!—a big bag of M&Ms.

She handed me one glass and sat down on the bench next to me, setting the open bag of delicious hard-shelled candy between us. "How are you holding up? I get the feeling you're holding back on us, Aubree. First, that pisses me off, and secondly, it doesn't surprise me. You do love the dress, right?"

Suddenly cold, I slowly rubbed my upper arms, my gaze riveted on the frosty glass of lemonade in my hand. "I adore the dress. Absolutely. It's so beautiful, and I am also very grateful that you guys took that task off the list. I think I waited and waited because I was worried I would make the wrong choice."

Setting the lemonade onto a small side table, I grabbed a handful of candy and popped a few into my mouth.

She turned toward me. River, who was always straightforward and blunt. I loved her like a sister, and the fact that she and I were going to be sisters-in-law was icing on the cake. That feeling doubled at the thought that Verity was in the same boat with us. My sweet friends were there for me through thick and thin.

And we would support our Outlaws through it all.

River squeezed my arm. "You put too much pressure on yourself," she said, then leaned back, eating more candy. "We're not totally home free. After veil, underthings, and shoe shopping we'll be a step closer."

Her voice dropped, her eyes dark, as I popped in more chocolate. "Booker was pretty much tied in knots when he was suckered into coming over to the house for this stupid drinking game."

I stopped chewing and groaned. The inflection of disgust in her voice heralded more Outlaw shenanigans. "Oh, God. I made him promise...?"

River laughed. "Oh, sugar, they're Outlaws. They can't help themselves." She shook her head. "Drunk fighting. All three of them were hammered on fruit punch moonshine with a black eye apiece. And plenty of cuts and bruises." Her eyes dancing, she said, "Booker was passed out cold. Geez, I bet Braxton punches hard."

Regardless of all the stuff I was dealing with, I rested my head back while my body shook. Those...*Outlaws*... OMG...what to do with them. I slapped my hand over my face, shaky laughter still bubbling. "He wisely didn't say anything about that on the phone. Smart man."

River laughed with me. "They suckered him good. Lured him with candy-flavored 'shine."

"He can't resist anything that has to do with red and Gummy Bears."

I lifted my head, my gaze connecting with the lingering humor, concern, and sympathy in River's eyes. I held her gaze for a split second, then closed my eyes, dragging my hair back, frustration and a sense of helplessness raging through me. I exhaled heavily and rubbed my eyes, trying to dig through the rubble of my mind.

"I messed up."

"So, won't be the first time, probably won't be the

last," she deadpanned.

"You know how I am."

"Yeah, organization personified. What did you do, schedule him into your calendar?" she said off the cuff.

When I bit my lip, she rolled her eyes, giving me an incredulous look. "Ohmigod...Aubree...."

"No, not that, but I always seemed to be putting him second. And, I guess when he didn't complain, I thought he was okay with it. O-chem is kicking my butt, and I have my sorority commitments, studying for my other classes, and my volunteer job. So many things to juggle. But I should never have juggled Booker. He's my life, River."

"Well, speaking from experience, I know what it's like to love like that. Brax is...everything, too. He's so wonderful, I would give up everything else for him."

"According to your parents you did that when you gave up modeling."

"Yeah, I know, but they can't complain. Brax's sauces are bringing in a hefty profit, and we're all reaping the benefits of his genius. I love my gallery so much, and being able to paint again is the best."

"I had no doubt."

"Okay then, Aubree, why don't you cut yourself some slack? Ease up on the self-chastisement and accept that even you..." She shook me. "Yes, even you make mistakes. Screw 'em. Mistakes are on the human continuum. We learn from them, and it makes us oh-so-much-smarter." She made a funny face at me and I laughed. "At least, that's what I tell myself. Besides, when you see Booker, the makeup sex will be...great."

I blushed and shoved some more M&Ms in my mouth, clinging to the thought of when I could be with him again.

"I'm going to play the interfering friend and give you some advice. Just get through the rest of the semester, leave the wedding preparations to me and Verity. All I need are the particulars for the flowers, wedding favors, and other details. I'll go over the list with you quickly before we leave tomorrow. Brax has the cake and the reception sewed up. Then you're free to sort out the personal stuff."

"You're just worried I'll turn into Bridezilla if you don't help me out. Raging through Suttontowne and leveling it into a wasteland."

"If Booker is anything like Boone and Brax, and I know he is, he's loyal to the end. He'll work out his own crap. I'm sure of it, Aubree. At the very least, it's because he loves you that you guys found each other in the first place. So buck up."

She hooked her arm around my neck, picked up a few M&Ms and shoved them into my mouth. "We'll eat ourselves sick on M&Ms and drink." I laughed around the mouthful and her blue eyes twinkled. "Oh, and by the way, I spiked your lemonade. We'll have our own drinking game."

I hooked my arm around her neck and did my own shoving of M&Ms. "Thank you for coming, River Pearl," I said quietly.

River grinned back at me with chocolatey teeth that made me laugh. "You're welcome, Breebree."

Booker

"Isn't that too high?" I said, backing up and looking at the rose. Braxton was working on another iteration of our wedding cake. I was currently looking over his shoulder. "Is something burning?" I asked as I sniffed the air.

Braxton sighed and whirled on me, shoving me out of

the way and heading toward the oven. He gave me a calculated look and pulled out more sponge cake. "It's just the extra batter on the pan getting toasty." He leveled a look that would have killed me dead in my sneakers if looks could kill. "Don't you have something better to do than come into my kitchen and drive me batty with your comments?"

"No, I don't. I miss—"

"If you so much as utter her name again with the word miss, I. Am. Going. To. Deck. You. It's only been a week."

"Geez, you're touchy."

"Booker, why don't you go see Ma? Catch up with her and Win. She can tell you all about her visit to New Orleans. Right?"

"You're trying to get rid of me."

"What was your first clue?"

"All right," I said, snatching up a generous amount of buttercream frosting and licking it off my finger. "Needs more butter," I said, smirking. Brax threw the spatula at me, but I ducked. "Ha! Missed."

"I'm warning you, huckleberry!"

"That rose is too high," I said quickly, then danced out of the kitchen and shut the door before he started throwing sharp objects like knives and cleavers.

Something heavy banged against the door as I heard a steam of Cajun French with my name mixed in.

"Aunt Heloise would wash your mouth out with soap," I yelled through the door.

"Booker!"

I chuckled. As much fun as this was, I agreed with Brax. I needed something to do so I would stop thinking about how much I missed Aubree. We'd talked on the phone a couple of times, but they were brief conversations, and didn't fill the empty hole in my gut.

Once in my GT, I drove over to my ma's house.

Getting out of the car, I walked up her flagstone path, picking a bunch of hydrangeas. As I entered the house, I could hear the buzz of a saw coming from the back while I wove through a maze of boxes and old Confederate stuff scattered everywhere around the kitchen and living room. I saw some old journals on the counter. I recognized them as the ones River Pearl had read that revealed what had happened with our ancestors.

"Ma?" There was no answer. I grabbed a vase for the flowers, and added water. After putting the bouquet on her island, I picked up one of the journals and immediately liked Duel's sweeping handwriting. I set it back down and thought maybe I should read them. I headed for the back, the screen door slapping as I passed through.

I approached her storage shed/antique display area and saw Win Sutton, shirtless and in a pair of worn jeans, running a band saw, a tool belt around his lean waist. I'd never seen him so casual. Win was usually a snappy dresser.

My ma was sitting not far from him, her eyes broadcasting her very...intimate thoughts. Not exactly what I wanted to know about my ma, but I was glad she was happy. The saw shut off and Win grinned at her. She ran her bare toe up his calf. "You know you're distracting me, sugar. I would get this done a lot faster without you over in the corner giving me the sultry eye."

"I can't help it. You are the one over there looking all carpenter sexy." She waggled her brows, tilting her head, giving him the once over. "Win, why don't we—"

I cleared my throat and my ma's head whipped around and she straightened, and I swear her face turned beet red. Win chuckled, but cut it off when she gave him a quelling look. Yeah, my ma had one helluva quelling look.

"Booker, so good to see you," Win said, reaching for a rag and wiping his neck and chest.

"We were just making some display cases."

"Ohhh, so that's what you were doing," I said, giving him a wink and hugging her, giving her a kiss on her flushed cheek. I shook his hand. "Looks more like making time to me."

She shoved me lightly. "Oh, Booker...hush. Now, what brings you here? Not that I'm complaining. I love to see my boy."

I gave her my best hangdog look. "Brax won't play with me. He kicked me out of his kitchen and took all his toys back."

She laughed. "Oh, my. That big ol' meanie. Well, he will have to go to bed without his supper tonight."

I laughed and said, "What's all this?"

"Oh, your momma has a notion to display some of that ol' Confederate stuff she has in the attic. She's also going to take your advice and open up her own antique shop. So, the display cases."

"That's great."

"Sugar, would you mind getting me some of your delicious lemonade? I've built up quite a thirst here."

She smiled and cupped his face, running her thumb over his cheekbone. He stared down at her, and I couldn't be happier that my ma was so...content and happy. I'd never let her see how I was also squirming with...embarrassment? She sashayed out of the shed and I shook my head.

As soon as she was out of hearing distance, Win approached me and indicated the chair. I sat down, but instead of taking the other chair near the work bench, he paced. "Everything okay, Win?"

He threw a look over his shoulder and reached into his pocket. "I wanted to talk to each of you boys separately." He cleared his throat. "It works out that you came home for your wedding early. I don't want to steal your thunder, and I'll wait a respectful time, but I want to ask your blessing to marry your momma."

I stood and offered him my hand. We shook and embraced, slapping each other on the back. "You have it." I respected him. Thought he was an upstanding guy for the way he stuck up for us, and for River Pearl and Braxton. My ma loved him. It was plain to see. He made her happy. What else mattered?

"You have the ring in your pocket, don't you?"

"I carry it around with me everywhere, terrified I'll lose it or she'll find it."

"Can I see it?"

He looked over his shoulder, but my ma was still busy. She must have gotten caught up in her old Confederate stuff.

He pulled out the box and I whistled. "That is a doozy."

"I want to talk to your brothers and then I'll—"

"What are you two whispering about...Win..." she said when she saw the ring box and the diamond nestled inside. He groaned. I smiled.

She had her arms loaded with those old journals. She set them down on a small table. Her expression was so vulnerable, so surprised. She looked to the ring, then to his face. "Yes," she said and threw herself into his arms.

He buried his face in her neck and held her tight. "Just like you, Evie, to not even give me a chance to ask," he groused.

She pulled away long enough to give him a sound kiss. "Ask if you want to, but the answer is going to be the same."

"I wanted to talk to all your sons before..."

"Oh, that is so sweet."

He shifted, then shook his head, grinning. "Will you marry me, Evangeline?"

"Yes, I will, Winchester."

He chuckled and slipped the ring on her finger.

I hugged my ma and said, "Congratulations." Looking at Win, I grinned. "Welcome to the family, Daddy."

A subtle look came over his face, and even though I was half joking, I could see he was affected by my acceptance. "Don't worry. Brax and Boone won't have any objections."

Win went back to his sawing and building. My ma pulled me aside and handed me Duel's journals. "Here, Booker, take these. Maybe you can...I don't know...write a memoir or something to commemorate your ancestor. It certainly is an interesting story, you have to admit."

"Hmmm, I do need something to do. I've been thinking about my next book, but hadn't made a decision yet." I tucked them under my arm and kissed her on the cheek. "Brax will be so disappointed when he finds out I have finally found something to do."

She chuckled, and I left as I heard the saw abruptly cut off.

Zoe Dawson

CHAPTER FIVE

Booker

I RAMBLED around a bit the next day. Aubree was able to call me while she was heading out to class, though our conversation was once again brief.

She reminded me about Dr. Rust's celebration, and I promised her I had the perfect gift for him. It had occurred to me only an hour before, but I'd already done some research and ordered it for him, putting a rush on it for Saturday delivery. I explained to the saleslady how important it was to get here on time, and she assured me it would be delivered. The other gift was purely for him.

Afterwards, I picked up those old journals and started reading, got totally into them, and an idea was born. I should have been finishing the half-done book in my series. But before I knew it, I had an outline, and I was feverishly working on something that was making my nerves jump with excitement.

For the next week I wrote nonstop, and by the time I got to the following weekend, I had completed a substantial but rough draft. I went through it one more time, took a centering breath, and sent it off to Lottie, jinglingly aware of being nervous for the first time in my writing life. I wanted her to love it. I did, was sure this was a good idea, but Lottie would tell me what she thought. She was always honest.

On the day of Dr. Rust's celebration, I pulled out my suit, knotted up my tie, and even shaved. Aubree would want me to look good. I drove over to the town hall where the party was being held, and saw Brax's truck was already there. People were converging on the hall, and when I walked in it was getting pretty loud.

Dr. Rust was sitting at one of the head tables talking to Rory Finnegan. He and Savannah Hawkins were currently the talk of the town. Savannah's momma was mad as an ol' wet hen that her daughter had defied her. I couldn't help smiling, remembering when Brax had come to Boone and me about Rory's mortgage, and why I'd been more than happy to contribute a third of the cost.

First, it would get that old, pushy, naggy lady's goat. She had been particularly nasty to my ma back when she was struggling as all get-out. Vengeance was certainly sweet, even if it was anonymous. Secondly, Rory had served our country, and was a great asset to my brother, Brax, as his bartender. He would be successful at his tattoo business. I could tell about people, and I was more than happy to contribute to that as well. The guy deserved a break.

I felt a kindred spirit with Rory, who'd snatched Savannah out of the upper crust of society, and proud of her for making the right choice.

Us bad boys had to stick together.

I went to settle at one of the seats, but Dr. Rust motioned me over. He smiled as I approached, and Rory turned to see who Dr. Rust was looking at. He smiled and shook the hand I offered. I greeted Savannah with a quick hug.

After small talk, Rory and Savannah left and sat down at a table over.

"Have a seat," Dr. Rust said. "Aubree emailed me that you would be attending in her stead. Thank you for that."

"Yes, sir. It was an honor to be asked. Aubree thinks very highly of you."

"How are that shoulder of yours and your head doing?"

He was referring to my gunshot wound from last summer, and the concussion thanks to Daniel Langston.

"I'm doing great. I had this great doctor."

He snorted. "Whose advice you ignored, but I understand. Young love and all." He waved his hand. "Aubree tells me you're getting married real soon."

"Two more weeks. It's coming up fast."

"You are a lucky man. You do realize that, I'm sure."

"Sir?"

"Marrying that gal. She's a keeper. I had an email from Dr. Palmer. She tells me that she offered Aubree the opportunity to speak at the AMA student's symposium." He took a sip of sweet tea and sat back, getting comfortable. "Short notice and all, but the scheduled speaker had to cancel. Anyway, she turned Dr. Palmer down. Would have been a nice bit of gold on her application, but it's clear Aubree has her priorities straight."

"She what?"

"Turned it down cold. It's only two days after your wedding." He sat forward, his weathered blue eyes intense. "Do you know the statistics for the likelihood of finding someone to take over a country practice?"

"No, sir."

"They aren't good. The fact that Aubree is planning to practice here is very good for Suttontowne. I would hate to leave them high and dry when I retire. It's a tough life, son. I'm on call seven days a week, rarely

65

take any type of vacation, and have to drive frequently to Lafayette for my rounds at the hospital, but I haven't ever regretted choosing to serve."

Things had settled down and the food was being dished out. I could smell Braxton's jambalaya. Aubree was going to be sorry she missed it, but it was also Dr. Rust's favorite dish.

"What do you do for a livin' son?"

"I'm a writer," I said absently, his words, the meaning of what Aubree had given up for me all whirling around in my head.

The doctor's brows rose. "One of them internet successes?"

"Yes, sir. I've done very well on the internet." I nodded. "How long have you been practicing?"

"Going on thirty-three years, and I don't talk too much about retiring, but the time will come. Tulane is very good about keeping a balance between city and country medicine. I like that, and it's why I'm happy to have students out here who want to shadow me. Aubree is a great addition to that school.

"You can make up your own mind about this, but I like the way she thinks of the patient as a whole person. Need that kind of thinking when you practice alone. I think she would have been a healer no matter where or when she was born. Being a woman is also to her advantage. I've never been too much of a touchy-feely doctor, but I think her patients will do well with her nurturing.

"When I think of Aubree, I think of a healer, because that's what she is. Now, you support her, you hear? She has a calling and a gift. Make sure she has a solid foundation so she can excel, stand by her. That's where the success comes in marriage. And, quite simply, Suttontowne needs her."

He smiled. "Ah, there she is. A sight for sore eyes."

A Perfect Wedding

I whipped around and my heart turned over. Aubree was making her way through the crowd. She smiled briefly for Dr. Rust, then her eyes were only for me. Her smile was only for me. I got up as she approached and she wrapped her arms around my neck and I breathed in her unique scent, holding onto her like she was my lifeline.

"Hello, my sweet Booker."

"Babe, I thought—"

"I have been working with Dr. Palmer on o-chem and feeling much better about it, so I decided to blow off my study session and my sorority function. This was more important," she leaned in close, her mouth against my ear and whispered, "I wanted to see you, be with you. I can't go another night without having you close to me."

"You're staying the night?"

"Yes, and some of tomorrow. I don't have to be back to New Orleans until late afternoon."

"Sweet," I breathed.

Just then Dr. Rust was called to the front of the room. I signaled one of Brax's waiters for a meal for Aubree while they presented Dr. Rust with his plaque, an engraved stethoscope, and a monogrammed lab coat. He would also have someone to cover him on the presenter's dime while he took a much-deserved vacation. Everyone cheered and gave him a standing ovation. Then the party broke up. Dr. Rust headed back to the table, and I looked at my watch.

"Sir, would you accompany us back to your office? Aubree and I have something for you."

"Oh, you shouldn't have done it, but I thank you."

We walked hand in hand, since I couldn't seem to let go of her. I couldn't wait to get her back home. When we turned onto the block leading to Dr. Rust's practice, I saw the delivery truck.

It stopped in front of the office and the driver got out.

"Hey, is the doc around?"

"He is now. What can I do for you, son?"

The driver looked down at his paperwork. "I have a delivery for a Dr. Rust."

"That's me. But, I wasn't expecting my medical supplies for at least another week."

"These aren't medical supplies. This here," he opened up the back, "is an x-ray machine. Where do you want it?"

Dr. Rust looked at us and then Aubree looked at me.

I shrugged. "You told me get him something nice."

She wrapped her arm around my waist and squeezed. "You are so generous and sweet, and kind."

"Shh," I said, "You'll ruin my rep."

She laughed. "Oh, we can't have that."

"Let me show you where to put it," Dr. Rust said, and was actually rubbing his hands and cackling while he scurried up the sidewalk.

We waited until the delivery guy had placed the machine exactly where the doc wanted it.

When the delivery guy left I thanked him. Then we walked back to find Doc just staring at the new machine. "This is going to save my patients a lot of trips."

I reached into my pocket. "Doc, the x-ray was for the practice. This is for you." I handed him the envelope.

He opened it and took a quick, indrawn breath. "This is so generous. I don't know what to say."

"I have heard enough talk on that bar stool at Outlaws how you wanted to fish marlin in the Keys. Now's your chance. When your replacement comes, you can get away. It's an open ticket."

"I've never flown first class in my life."

"There's a first time for everything. Enjoy your trip."

I shook his hand and Aubree hugged him. "Thank you for everything you've done for the town and for me."

He nodded, still a bit overcome.

I ushered Aubree out of there. I kissed her just shy of the front door, her mouth eager, lush and moist, and I wanted to sink into her and stop thinking, stop analyzing and just feel her.

I kept her next to me until we got into my car. The drive through the bayou made her sigh, and I could tell she was glad to be home.

She leaned over the console and kissed my face, trailing more kisses down my neck.

I drove with one hand, the other in her soft hair.

Finally at the house, she came around the car, and we stood in the dark garage, kissing each other like there was no tomorrow.

"I missed you, so much."

"I missed you more," she said.

We went into the house, and just inside the kitchen stopped as she pulled me against her and kissed me deeply. The moon glowed throughout the room, and I stared down into her eyes and felt the power of our connection, her gaze setting off a crazy, wild need in my gut. A fierce longing spilled into my bloodstream, a longing to touch her, to be held and touched back, to feel her warmth and softness around me.

I pushed my thoughts away, pushed everything away, especially the pain of the thoughts Dr. Rust had dredged up...thoughts that were going to take me some time to sort out.

I let it go for now because I needed her. Besides, it was fundamental. We always seemed to be in a mess.

#

Aubree

I was finally where I wanted to be, but I couldn't

ignore the fact that Booker was wrestling with his own uncertainties. What a pair we were. Taking his face between my hands, I kissed him with all the love and longing welling up inside me.

His chest expanded as he inhaled raggedly; then his arms came around me in a crushing embrace as he took what I offered. His jaw flexed beneath my hand as he moved his mouth against mine, the thoroughness of his hot, wet kiss setting off a wild frenzy in my belly.

Shifting his hold, Booker caught me around the hips, drawing me flush against his pelvis, and my breath caught on a rough sob, the surge of sensation making my lungs falter. He tightened his arms around me, holding me with familiar fierceness, his mouth hungry. His need merged with my own, and I went all soft and willing in his arms, a liquid weakness spreading through me.

With a shuddering intake of air, he dragged his mouth away. He stared down into my eyes, his gaze offering a strange mix of contradictions. Verbal silence, but silent communication. Distance, but a strange kind of closeness. I drew on his silent strength, repeatedly trying to reassure myself that everything would be all right.

"I love you, Booker. Don't ever doubt that." I cupped his face between my hands and said fiercely. "*Ever.*"

He looked away, the muscles in his throat convulsing, and this man just stripped me bare. How could I ever have defenses against him? He was a treasure.

"Ah, *geezus*, Aubree," he whispered, his face contorting with raw emotion. "I don't doubt it. I just got...sidetracked. I thought I had somehow lost you."

"No, never."

He crushed me even closer.

"It's okay, babe," he said softly.

A Perfect Wedding

I tightened my hold on him and made a low, urgent sound, a crazy kind of fear claiming me. I pushed off his jacket and unknotted his tie, brushing my mouth against his. With urgency, I undid all the buttons and pushed the shirt off him, then stroked his lean muscles all the way to his waistband.

It was as if he felt the same thing, and with a hoarse growl, he tipped my head back and found my mouth, his savage kiss tasting of tears and pain and fear-driven desperation.

For me, there was a taste of hope in the way he kissed me. I latched onto it, because I trusted in Booker, trusted him with my life, with my heart, with my very soul. He dragged his hand up my back, molding us together in a crushing hold, his other hand immobilizing my head as his mouth turned hot, hungry, and ravaging.

Widening his stance, Booker dragged me up into the cradle of his thighs, the hard ridge of his flesh meshing with my softness, and suddenly I couldn't breathe, couldn't think, for the thick, pulsing urgency swelling within me.

Booker groaned and dragged his mouth away, his breathing ragged as he lifted my hips up and against his, a violent shudder coursing through him. With his merciless hold fusing us body to body, I wrapped my legs around him, giving him full access to the heat denied him by the barrier of our clothing. His breathing harsh against my ear, he gripped me around my hips, locking me against him, his body thrusting, driving, urgent against mine. I clung to him, my senses sucked into a mindless need, and I dragged my hands up his bare back, my fingers digging into his straining muscles as I twisted my body against his, trying to bring him closer.

He carried me over to our couch and set me down,

delving under my skirt, ripping off my panties and unbuckling his belt.

He pushed me back on the couch, and I was vividly aware of the heat and hardness of his honed body.

Awash in a whole storm of emotion, tightened my hold on him, murmuring his name again and again. He came down on top of me, and I cried out, his weight heavy in the apex of my thighs. Sensations and emotions raged through me, and I flexed my legs, thrusting up against him, mindlessly trying to get him inside me.

He met my thrust and slipped inside with a hoarse groan, tucking one arm under my hips and he pulled out and entered me fully in one savage thrust.

I shrieked with delight and arched against him, an incoherent frenzy claiming me. His fingers tangling in my hair, Booker held my head still and covered my mouth with a punishing kiss that blasted into me like a loaded grenade, breaking me, stripping me, making me thoroughly his again.

He thrust into me again with a fragmented groan. Dragging his mouth away from mine, he buried his face against the curve of my neck, a hard, wild urgency claiming him, incinerating the last of his restraint. And then there was no holding back. Raw and violent. Engulfing. Without a trace of gentleness, he came, his body jackknifing, shuddering, his head thrown back.

I rode out that storm with him, rode it out until he finally was spent, collapsed on top of me.

For several long moments we lay there while I just absorbed the bliss of his skin against mine, the warmth of him, his presence. My fingers played in that gorgeous, shaggy hair, heated silk.

Without a word, he got up, kicked off his pants and underwear, picked me up in his arms and walked to the bedroom. I stripped off the rest of my clothes and we settled against the cool sheets.

The sounds of the bayou settled around me, and it was here where I had fallen for my Outlaw, in this house where he had taken my virginity, given me my first taste of womanhood, and become my first heartbreak, and my first and only love.

"Come back to New Orleans with me, Booker," I begged. Expelling a long sigh, he slipped one arm under my head and the other around my midriff, drawing me securely into the curve of his body. Thrown into emotional overload, I tried to turn in his arms, but he held me fast, the arm around my middle locking me against him.

"I think I need to stay here. Let you close out the semester. Things seem like they might be going better."

I nodded, trying to ease the nearly crippling clot of emotion. I smoothed my hand across the back of his, my voice breaking with strain when I started to speak. "Booker, I'm so sorry."

Shifting his arm, he pressed his thumb against my mouth, his chest expanding heavily against my back, his voice very gruff when he spoke. "I'm sorry, too."

I knew Booker had been pushed to the wall, because I needed him to understand and support me, no matter how busy and crazy I got, and he was struggling with that.

Knowing that made me feel very small—because I had given him reason to doubt me. But I wasn't sure how to reassure him, or how to help him get through the battle he was waging. When it came to my intelligent, cerebral Outlaw, it was best to leave him be. Let him come to his own conclusions. I didn't want Booker to ever, ever be dishonest with himself, no matter how much it hurt, no matter how things played out between us.

Tightening my hold on his hand, I closed my eyes,

the awful ache in my throat too big to handle, grateful he was at least trying.

The thought of making a choice between medicine and Booker was like a twisting, tug-of-war pain in my chest. I'd stopped kidding myself a long time ago. Reality was harsh, but that's where we all had to live. My first dose of that still haunted a set of bleachers, the second lay on Old Magnolia Road and the third happened when Daniel kidnapped us.

Where I would experience the next dose. I wasn't sure.

He would always have to be true to himself.

My gorgeous, strong, unwavering Outlaw.

I knew he would always be true to me. Always be honest with me when he was ready to tell me his thoughts.

Always.

#

Aubree

Booker was up when I awoke the next morning. The scent of him, of our lovemaking, still clung to the sheets, and I rolled over onto my stomach, every shred of tension dissipated.

I was going to trust Booker. It felt so good to wake up relaxed and rested.

Sighing, I rolled over onto my back, making a mental list of the things I had to do in the next week before I could come back here, finish our wedding preparations, and get hitched. Dr. Palmer had been more than equal to the task of helping me with o-chem. She asked me point blank if I had a mental block about o-chem, because without a passing grade, I couldn't get into med school. She wanted to know if I was subconsciously sabotaging myself. I couldn't sleep when I got home after that discussion, and thought long and hard about what she said.

Then I tightened my resolve and faced that accusation head on. Discovered I was being sabotaged by the fear of failure. I faced it. Brought it out in the open and dealt with it. There was only one way forward, and that was by passing o-chem. My final was this week and I felt ready...shaky, but determined to do my best and let the chips fall where they may.

Realizing I was postponing the inevitable, I reluctantly hauled myself out of bed and got dressed. When I wandered into the living room, I saw Booker in the kitchen. He was drinking a cup of coffee and staring out into the bayou.

He turned when he heard me enter. "Ah, time you woke up and smelled the coffee."

"When I woke up, it certainly wasn't coffee I smelled."

His cup stopped halfway to his mouth, and he stared at me, the sudden narrowing of his eyes indicating he knew exactly what I was talking about. His gaze fixed on me. He raised the mug to his mouth and took a sip of coffee, a glimmer of humor in his eyes. "Hot. Very hot."

Even with the knot of concern still turning in my stomach, I laughed. "You are such an Outlaw, still the astronaut of awesome."

"Nice to know my...ah...black hole still works."

I laughed again, and went over to him and slipped my arms around his waist.

"Tell me what you've been up to."

He took a breath. "I started a new book. Lottie has it now. She hasn't responded to my email yet, and it's killing me."

"You finished your book already?"

"No, I haven't finished it yet. This idea just kinda came out of the blue."

Really, what is it about?"

"My family saga. A fictionalized version of it, anyway. My attempt to write our history and commemorate Duel Outlaw. A memoir seemed boring to me. This was my answer."

"It sounds interesting. I can't wait to read it."

There was an imperceptible lightening in his eyes, and the taut set of his mouth eased into a soft smile. "I also heard back from the producer. They are optioning my first three books for a film."

Not wanting him to see how disquieted I was to see him so unhappy and not know how to fix it, I smiled back, overjoyed for his success. "Are you serious?" I threw my arms around his neck and pressed my face against his rough jaw. "That is sensational. I'm so proud of you."

The tension around his mouth easing a little, he gave me that wonderful, patented Outlaw grin, and it bolstered me.

"Just out of curiosity," I began slowly, knowing this was the right moment, "have you figured out the honeymoon stuff yet?""

"No, not yet. Why?"

I bit my lip and smiled. "Why? Seven whole days of nothing but Booker? Are you crazy? I want to know where we're going."

His eyes twinkled and I liked that so much better. "I'm still working on it."

"Oh, God. You're killing me."

After a while, I said, "I've got to get going."

He nodded and drove me into town, where I got into my car. Through my open window he brushed his hand down my arm. "You know where to find me if you need me."

He bent down and gave me one last, lingering kiss.

If I needed him...If I needed him...I wondered how to

make sure he knew, to his bones, how much I did.

I put the car in gear and drove away, experiencing the strangest feeling in my stomach. I knew that parting comment was meant to reassure me. But what was unsettling me even more was the single touch. Whatever was bothering him, it was chewing him up inside.

I slammed on the brakes and I saw Booker watching me. Throwing the car into park, I opened the door and jumped out, breaking into a run. I got to him and threw my arms around his neck. "I need you, so much. Tell me you know that. I need you."

"I do now," he said holding me just as tight, and the terrible feeling in my stomach went away.

Zoe Dawson

CHAPTER SIX

Booker

STAYING in Suttontowne while Aubree drove away was the right move. Aubree tied me up in knots, distracted me, made me crazy. I needed to do some heavy thinking, needed to get my head and heart to mesh.

Dr. Rust's revelations about being married to a country doctor, about what Aubree deserved and needed, would not leave me alone. Even as I said goodbye to her, I struggled with what he'd said, and was pretty sure I had only seen the tip of the iceberg. That Aubree's journey to becoming a doctor wasn't going to just limit our time for the next six years, in the end she was going to be the person Suttontowne relied on the most.

That meant I would have to sacrifice my time with her.

It hit me like a ton of bricks.

Aubree had a calling, a gift.

And I had to share her.

I didn't know if I could handle it.

But the alternative was even more devastating.

Losing her wasn't an option.

I wrestled with the concept, thinking that I had been selfish and petty. She was doing something for the common good. Something wholly generous and self-sacrificing. It was bigger than both of us.

It was our major issue, and now I realized why it was going to be a difficult discussion. Why she was nervous. She would be back in a week, and I was struggling with our future.

I had to do some real soul-searching, some deep, deep thinking. Because I would not commit myself to Aubree by a half measure. I would have to commit to her wholly, passionately, without reservations. To her and her choice of profession.

The thoughts shook my very foundations, and I trembled with them.

As the dust of her leaving settled, my cell rang.

Lottie.

My palms got instantly sweaty.

"Booker, are you free right now?"

"Yes. Why?"

"Why? *The book.* Come over here. We need to talk."

"All right. I'm in town, so I'll be right there."

I disconnected the call and my stomach jumped. Her tone was clipped and...seemed strange. Did she hate it and needed to tell me that in person? Usually Lottie didn't pull any punches.

When I pulled up to her house, I barely had a chance to knock before she opened the door. She looked disheveled, as if she hadn't slept, and I hadn't ever seen Lottie that way before. She was like Aubree. Always put together.

"Get in here." She grabbed my T-shirt and dragged me inside. She paced and ran her hands through her hair.

"Geezus," I said. "Was it that bad?"

She whirled on me. "What? No. My God, Booker, this

is...this is magnificent. If this doesn't hit the *Times,* you will have been robbed." She paced, then whirled again. "Do you have any more?"

"Um...no...that's just a rough draft."

"I want more. I stayed up all night reading it. I need some more right now. When can you have this ready?"

"I'm getting married." I had to take a calming breath.

Shit. I was getting *married*, and I still had to work out all these jumbled issues and confused thoughts about commitment and sacrifice. Hard, important decisions, not to be taken lightly.

Finally I said, "I have some summer plans brewing in my head. I don't know. Maybe the fall." I smiled feeling a lot lighter. "So you really liked it?"

"I loved it. The characterizations of Duel and Amy are so good. The writing is lush and heart-wrenching. How many books do you have planned?" The enthusiasm in her voice also lit up her eyes.

"Honestly, I don't know. I got this idea from my ma and those old journals. I know I want to tell the whole story, maybe even up to present day. Fictionalized, of course."

"Well, do your best to get this one done and polished ASAP. I'll edit it as soon as it's finished."

I stood there with the knowledge that this woman had been a part of my life. Some of the best part. My affection for her swelled to almost maternal proportions, and with a start I realized that I loved my soon-to-be mother-in-law.

All the conflicting things I was feeling were a tangled up mess, and the thought of disappointing her gave me the same kind of sick, squirmy feeling I got when I thought about disappointing my ma.

I grabbed her around the neck and hugged her to me, my voice thick. "Thank you, Lottie. I haven't ever told you how much you've influenced my life. How much it means to me. I believed in my brothers and helped them because you believed in me so strongly. I...love you, Lottie."

She wrapped her arms around me immediately, tightening her embrace. "Oh, Booker, I have never told you how thankful I am for what you did that day on Old Magnolia Road. If it wasn't for your courage, my daughter...Aubree would have... You saved her twice."

"Technically, I saved her the first time. You and your shotgun saved her the second. Saved us both."

"You are being humble. You didn't hesitate to throw your body over hers. I saw that, Booker, and I'll never forget it. I love you, too. I am so happy to become a part of your family, and have you become a part of ours. I couldn't have dreamed up a better man for Aubree. You'll keep her on her toes...and promise me you'll make sure she has fun."

I nodded.

"We'll gladly give her away to you without reservations."

"I promise never to let her down, and fun is my middle name."

"I know you won't, because there is such a strong character there," she tapped my chest, "and integrity in spades."

I heard footsteps on the stairs and the wry voice of the sheriff. "I'll give you a running start, Booker, while I go fetch my shotgun."

Lottie's laughter was light while we let go of each other, mildly embarrassed, and I stepped back and looked up at him.

He smiled. "You kept my wife up all night, and she hasn't stopped talking about you and that book. I'm jealous. I still might get my shotgun."

"Yes, sir. How much of a running start were you going to give me?"

A Perfect Wedding

Booker

My fingers were flying across the keyboard, and I was in the zone when I heard footsteps coming down the hall. Brax popped into view with Boone standing right behind him. Both of them had the Outlaw grin in plain sight.

"This can't be good," I said. "What do you two stooges have up your sleeves?"

"That makes you the third stooge."

"I can't help it, it's in our genes."

They both laughed. "Pack an overnight bag, huckleberry. This here is a kidnapping for your bachelor party."

"Ah, are you kidding me? I'm not going to any strip joint."

"Nope, there's no strip joint. We have more class than that."

I laughed and eyed them, but the grinning didn't disappear.

I sighed, thinking this wasn't such a good idea.

Hours later I wanted to punch Brax in the face, but his face was messed up enough. I leaned my head back against the concrete of the very secure jail cell. "So tell me, Moe and Larry. What is your plan now?"

I rolled my head to look at them.

"Bail. Getting out of jail card?" Boone suggested with a raised brow.

"Who should I call?"

"Please don't call Verity," Boone groaned.

"No way am I calling River Pearl. She'll rip me a new one."

"Well to be fair, Brax, you meant well."

"Yeah, lot of good that did us. We got arrested for it, and that guy had a helluva right hook."

"He was cheating. You had to speak up," Boone said. "Please call Breebree. She'll fix all my booboos and not yell at me."

"Yeah, Aubree. Call her. She's more reasonable."

"Hey, you guys. Your phone call?" The cop came to the cell and I rose. "Yes, sir. Thank you." I stepped out of the cell when he released the lock and opened it for me. I walked with him to the bank of phones and picked up the receiver. It was 3am, and I could only hope that Aubree was studying and she had left her phone on.

I dialed as the cop stood behind me. She picked up on the first ring. "Hey, Booker. What are you doing up so late?"

"Um...Aubree...I need you to...ah...come down to the New Orleans..." I pinched the bridge of my nose, a headache rising menacingly in the back of my head, "...jail."

I could hear the stunned shock on the other end of the line in the silence that followed my request. "What? What did you just say?"

She was really making me repeat it. "Jail, babe. We're in jail. Bring the checkbook."

"*Jail!*" she shrieked. "What...never mind. I'll be right there."

"I ain't going anywhere." I hung up and looked at the stoic cop, who gave me a tight smile, as if to say *that's right, buddy.*

Back in the cell, Brax and Boone looked even worse. There was blood on Boone's shirt, Brax's shirt was torn, and he had a bruise forming under his eye. I had a split lip and my nose felt swollen.

I sat down next to them, weary to the bone. "Thanks so much guys for a memorable bachelor party."

"Booker, Braxton, and Boone Outlaw, you're free to go."

"Wow, that was fast," Boone said. "What did Aubree do, fly here?"

We left the cell and headed out into the police station. A man was standing there waiting for us. "Hello guys, I'm Jeff, the manager at Harrah's. Sorry for the mix-up, and for y'all getting caught up in this. Several of my dealers told me what happened and vouched for you guys. Something ugly could have happened if you hadn't stepped in. All charges against you three have been dropped, and I thank you for doing the right thing. Your hotel stay is comped, and you are always welcome back to any of our hotel and casinos at half price." He handed us each a card.

We all shook his hand and just before he left, Aubree bustled through the front door. Our eyes met, and the worry and tenderness I saw there hit me hard in the heart. I loved the way she trusted me. The way she knew this had to be some kind of misunderstanding. It was all in her face.

Brax nudged me. "She's something, Book."

"Yeahhh," Boone said. "Our Breebree."

She rushed over, hugging each of us, and while the story unfolded she sympathized and teased us relentlessly. Once we were back at our hotel, she tended to Brax first, because he had taken most of the beating from the man who wanted to swindle the casino with his slick con game.

I watched her as she gently cleaned his cuts, thoroughly checked his bruises and asked him questions about his head. Then repeated it all over again with Boone, because I insisted he go before me. And it hit me as hard as that baseball bat had to my head.

That girl so got to me.

Hours later, sober, bruised and battered, we left Aubree in New Orleans as we headed home. My thoughts were a jumbled mess all the way back to Suttontowne. Still besieged with my own emotions, the enormity of marriage and commitment, the uncertainty of the future, I was tearing myself up with this struggle about what I wanted, what I could handle, and what we needed separately and as a couple. Could we make it if she became a doctor? Was I willing to give her up to other people, share her with her ridiculous work ethic and work hours?

I needed perspective, needed insight, but all I could feel was confusion. Was it even conceivable that I could actually make the decision that this wouldn't work for me? Was I that selfish? All these thoughts swirled while I half-listened to my brothers murmurs as I reclined in the back seat while I thought about how Aubree and I hurtled toward a collision course of what I wanted and what she wanted and what we could agree on.

Brax dropped Boone off, and I expected him to take me home, but instead he drove over to the wharf near Imogene's. "Walk with me," he said.

We bypassed the wood planking and jumped down to the water's edge. He picked up some stones and started to skip them. The moon was high and shed quite a bit of light.

"I know what's eating at you."

"How the fuck do you know that?"

"I figured it out tonight."

"Okay, enlighten me." I was so irritated and skeptical. I, mean, this was Brax. I might have even punched him if he didn't look so banged up.

"Get your fucking head out of your ass. Stop trying to be a goddamned knight to her. Be a guy who loves her. She doesn't want you to be perfect, Booker. Talk to her. Get mad at her. Fight with her. Your love can handle that."

I literally couldn't talk. I felt like I had swallowed my tongue.

"River and I fight all the time. Well," he shrugged, "mostly 'cause she's contrary." He skipped a stone, his voice full of his amusement. "But, she knows I'm hard to get along with, mostly a bastard. And you know something? That's okay, because I'm just being little ol' ornery me."

I gaped at him and he reached out and closed my mouth with a flick of his wrist. My teeth clacked together.

He sighed. "Booker, love isn't about the big picture. Sure, this wedding, the house you bought, the commitment—all big picture. You're projecting and panicking about not having enough time with her because of this doctoring thing. But, man..." he squeezed my shoulder and his face got serious and I have never respected him more, "where love sits and lives is the little things like holding her hand if she's afraid of needles, like covering her up when she's sleeping, like putting your arms around her because she makes your heart thump when you look at her, and like when you open your eyes in the morning and the first thing you want to see are her eyes looking back at you. The kind of look that makes you feel...alive. It lives in the blood, sweat, and tears of every moment you give to her. Make them count. Because love is in the details and those details make you a beautiful big picture."

"Geezus," I said. "Are you channeling Boone?"

"Nope, he's an amateur."

"Brax..."

"No, Book. There isn't anything else. Love is sacrifice and opportunities. River, she's my present and my future. Is Aubree yours?"

He handed me my keys, and left me to ponder as I heard the sound of a car and saw River step out, waiting for him. When he climbed the hill, they kissed, he got into the car and drove off.

#

Aubree

I stood outside my o-chem classroom with my back against the wall. The test was finally over, and it had been my last exam. I was sure I had done well in my other classes, but I still had anxiety over whether or not I passed this class.

Dr. Palmer had been instrumental...in getting me over this hump. With resonance orbitals, reaction mechanisms, mass spectroscopy, and infrared spectroscopy still swirling in my brain, I walked to my car. I had packed up everything I would need for the wedding and honeymoon the night before. We would most likely be spending the summer in Suttontowne, and I was okay with that. I missed the bayou, my friends, my mom, my home town, and I missed Booker most of all.

I had faith in him, but I was still on edge. I felt the sharpness of it, an edge that had been building for months.

I chuckled at his and the trips' botched attempt at a bachelor party. Those...Outlaws. What was I supposed to do with their shenanigans? Love them, I supposed, since I couldn't do anything else.

The two-hour trip went by quickly, and I was pulling into our driveway before I knew it. Booker's car wasn't there, and I guessed he must be handling last-minute wedding stuff, so I got busy moving almost everything into the house, where I would spend the night before we left, but leaving my small overnight bag and wedding stuff in the car. I was going to be staying with River Pearl until our wedding night.

Part of the traditional fun was getting us all charged with anticipation by waiting to make love.

My cell rang and I saw it was Brax. "What's up?"

"Are you here yet?"

"Yes, just pulled in."

"Great. Can you come over to Outlaws? I have some last-minute menu questions, and I want you to approve the cake."

"You're done with the cake?"

"Sorta. This one is my last attempt. I think I have it right. But I want you to be completely happy with it."

Tamping down my impatience to see Booker and talk to him—finally talk to him—I agreed and headed over to Outlaws. After the flurry of phone calls from River Pearl, Verity, my momma, and Evie for the last three weeks, plus our fun shopping day to get my veil, shoes, and lingerie, and our completely tame bachelorette party, not to mention my exhaustion over o-chem, sorority duties and volunteer job, I was running on fumes.

I just wanted to see Booker.

I waved to Rory, who was behind the bar, and saw the afternoon lunch crowd was just heating up. I pushed through the swinging doors and into the kitchen. Brax was at the counter plating up some orders, and he smiled at me as I came through the door.

I smiled back, but my frustration was about to boil over, and I just wanted to get this over with. It took him another ten minutes to handle his orders, then Martha took over with a quick hug for me.

"Okay, sorry about that. Been busy all day. It's in the walk-in freezer." I followed him and when he opened the door, I snapped. "The roses are supposed to be purple, Brax! Not lavender. If I had wanted lavender roses, I would have asked for them! Why are they all spread out? Wasn't this supposed to be tiered?"

Brax froze and turned to look at me. I clamped my hand over my mouth and lost it. Tears flooded my eyes. "I'm so sorry, ohmigod..." I bolted from the freezer and headed right out the back door. I plopped down on the steps and buried my face against my knees. Sobbing.

I heard the door open and close and felt someone settle next to me.

"I am going to tell you what I told Booker."

I took a shuddering breath and looked at him.

"Get your fucking head out of your ass."

"What...?" I sputtered.

"Aubree. You do too damn much. Lighten your load. The world isn't going to end and the whole damn foundation of the civilized world isn't going to collapse. Make time for Booker. Plain and simple. He's the most important person in your life, show him that he is. That's so goddamned easy."

My mouth fell open and he gently closed it with his index finger. Then he proceeded to blow my mind with this lecture about how love isn't a big picture, but in the details. He just waded through my crap in hip boots and nailed it on the head.

"Don't you know that Booker is afraid of not being your knight in shining armor? He's a freaking Boy Scout, our moral compass, and the brains of this outfit. But sometimes he can be so damn stoo-pid and so can you, Ms. Summa Cum Ladeda. It's bad enough that he avoids his feelings because of our childhood shit with our daddy. He has to work through that and I'm sure he will. This isn't about goddamned roses, Aubree, or tiers. My brother's been in love with you since the sixth grade. Now, come with me, dry your eyes and try some of my fucking delicious cake. I decided to go with a grouping instead of tiers, more interesting. But I took out all the calories just for you."

When I just stared at him. He sighed, hauled me to my feet, took me back to the walk-in freezer, forked up a piece of cake, and shoved it in my mouth.

"It's delicious," I mumbled. "You are so right. About the cake and about Booker."

"Don't look so shocked."

"I'm sorry, Brax." He wiped away my tears with his thumb. "I just want to see Booker."

He shoved a plate in my hands. "Tell me it's as if angels made it, and then go find him."

I picked up the fork. There were four slices on the plate. "This one is the topper," Brax said, pointing to the one on the left. "That's almond cake with raspberry filling."

I forked up a bite and tasted it. It hit my tongue like raspberry fire, the cake melted in the flame and it all blended into an exquisite taste. I closed my eyes and hummed. When I opened them, Brax was smiling.

"Ohmigod. What...? Raspberry liqueur."

"Ha! I'm a redneck. Guess again."

"No, you didn't."

"Sure did."

"Raspberry moonshine?"

He just chuckled and nodded. "This is devil's food."

I tasted that sample, and hummed again. "You put butterscotch chips in it. Scrumptious."

"And, for this one, lemon cake."

"Oh, God, the frosting, Brax...."

"Sprinkled with a sugary lemon syrup for added flavor. And the last one is white cake."

"Just as delicious, simple and classic."

"Are you happy?"

"Yes, you worked so hard."

"I know how to handle it." He leaned over and nudged me with his shoulder. "It'll be our little secret." He grabbed my chin with plain ol' Outlaw mischief glinting in his eyes. "Now, can we go over these menu details, please, and afterward I'll be a nice guy and tell you exactly where you can find that huckleberry you're marryin'."

"Thanks again, Brax. And I'm very sorry I blew up at you." I kissed him full on the mouth, and his surprised grunt along with the wry look on his face was worth it.

Then he recovered, a grin spreading across his face, nudged me again, and said, "Wow, all I got from Booker was a dumb-shit look. But, we'll keep this our little secret, too."

After we handled all Brax's questions, he told me Booker was over at Evie's, hauling stuff out of her shed so she could renovate the structure. They were taking everything to a storage unit for the time being.

Before I went over there, I had to stop at the store and then go home. Prepare something for Booker. When I pulled up to his momma's, I got kinda lost in the view. Stripped to the waist, Booker was standing with his arms braced on a table as he looked into the back of the truck, the muscles across his chest and broad shoulders thrown into sharp relief, glistening with sweat. Unable to take my eyes off him, I watched him talk to whoever was in the truck, assuming it was Boone.

He flashed a smile and gave the unknown person his middle finger. Ah...yeah, it was Boone.

My God I loved them all, these Outlaws, so much, especially the way they loved each other, their potent and unbreakable brotherhood and family ties.

There was no doubt that my husband-to-be was hot, but there was this pure aura of masculinity, sexual intensity that charged up his charisma, and it wasn't his knee-melting face or that leanly muscled body, it was Booker's confidence in who he was. There were never any half measures with my man, and there never would be. He gave all of himself to everything he did.

A frisson of nerves sent fingers of unease through me. It was time to get his issues out in the open, and then we would go from there. Knight in shining armor. Huh.

He glanced over, then did a double-take, and the smile that lit up his face was pure Outlaw and wholly for me. He said something to the person in the truck, and I opened my car door as he started over.

"Sugar," he said, reaching me. "I didn't expect you until later. Why didn't you just call me?"

"I'm tired of talking to you on the phone. I want to talk to you in person."

He touched my hair, tucking some of it behind my ear, tracing the rim. "How did the finals go? O-chem?"

"All of them and, yes, even o-chem went well. I want to talk to you...privately."

"Okay, we have one more load. I can be back at the house in, say, about thirty minutes."

I leaned forward, and he murmured, "I'm all sweaty," but I didn't pay him any heed. Wrapped my arms around him and kissed him. Boone looked around the truck and waved. I waved back.

He opened his mouth on mine and dragged me against him. "I'll see you soon," I said as we parted and I got back into my car.

#

Booker

I entered the house and Aubree was sitting on my piano stool. She looked...angry.

"You're thirty minutes late. We need to talk, and yet you didn't show up."

I opened my mouth to tell her that we got a flat tire, but she bulldozed right over me.

"You want to know something else?" she said her eyes narrowing. "You're too easy on me. Moody. A doormat. Always hide your real feelings behind humor. You live in your head, a tortured place. You have enough information and ammunition in that brain of yours to be impossible to argue with... You hold back on me!"

"Wait a damn, minute...what the fuck, Aubree? You're a workaholic, don't make time for what's important, worry too much about whether you're good enough, and you're a freaking know-it-all and are more freaking moody than I am. You hog the covers, refuse to order dessert, and then eat mine." I was breathing fire as I crossed the room and got right in her face and she didn't budge an inch.

"Anything else?" she said, bunching my dirty, greasy shirt in her hands as if she could care less about getting messy and brushing her mouth over mine. I was confused and felt elated, hot, bothered, worn out, and a storm was bubbling to the surface. Weren't we fighting? Didn't she just attack me without provocation?

"Yes, I want fucking time with you! I don't care what it takes! I want you to drop something."

"Ooh, you're very sexy when you're demanding. Okay. I'm going to pass the sorority stuff over to the other girls and bow out. I've told them, and they totally understand."

"What...I'm...Are you...Arrrgghhh."

"You don't have to hold back with me, Booker. Knights are boring. You're not, especially with your blue eyes blazing like that. It's pretty hot. I think it's rather stirring arguing with you."

"Huh?" I looked down at her, my man stuff getting way too tangled up with her woman stuff for my obviously blood-starved big brain to handle. "You did that on purpose." Then it dawned on me. "Brax, he told you."

"Yes, and how is it that your biggest, darkest secret has to be spilled by your brother?"

I shrugged. "I don't know. I find it hard to deal with negative emotions when it comes to you."

"Booker. You don't expect me to be perfect. Do you?"

I wrapped my hands around her waist. "No, of course not."

"Then why are you expecting the same thing for yourself?"

I took a breath. "Between you and Brax, I'm feeling pretty stoo-pid."

"You're not stupid, sugar. You are so caring and thoughtful that sometimes your needs get lost. Tell me what you want when you want it. I won't break. And I won't leave you. Ever.

"Okay, I think I can handle that."

"Come with me. I got a game we can play."

I groaned. "It's not a drinking game is it?"

"No, it's a kissing game."

A smile split across my face. "Oh, I like it better already."

"Yeah, and we've taken care of duking it out, so we won't need to fight anymore. At least not today."

She dragged me to the bathroom and I stopped dead. Candles, a bubble bath, and...poster paper all over the walls with handwritten passages on them. I took a breath.

Sometimes the things we can't change...end up changing us. The Colonel watched Duel Outlaw swing on the end of the rope and knew what had transpired here made him someone he didn't recognize.

Amy had the eyes. Those eyes. The kind of eyes that can look right through any attempt to hide, to the best a person has to offer. Twenty percent devil, eighty percent angel. Down to earth. No fear about getting her hands a little dirty with the mess that was life. For Duel, it was love at first sight.

"These are from my book."

"I read it and was blown away."

"How did you get a copy?"

"My momma couldn't stop talking about it. Talked

her into sharing her copy, and I couldn't put it down. The way you tell it between the past and the present was genius."

Brax had been right, love was about the details and Aubree's details made my life so rich. "You got the detail talk, too."

"Yeah, Brax. He needs a raise."

I laughed. "I agree, but don't tell the fathead that."

She snagged the hem of my T-shirt, dragging it over my head. Then her hands were on my jeans and she pushed them off. "Get in the tub."

I climbed in and closed my eyes, quickly getting sleepy from the warm water and the relief of stress. The water sloshed and my eyes popped open to find Aubree stepping in.

"Booker, I know this year has not been easy. It's been a revelation for both of us. My schedule…"

"Sucked, pissed me off, left me high and dry, made me crazy. Plus I was lonely for most of it."

I leaned forward to say more, and she rubbed her thumb over my mouth, her expression serious, a warning that I was not to argue with her. I stared at her for a moment, then let my breath go in a sigh of assent. I smoothed my hand up her arm, dulled by both mental and physical exhaustion.

"I wasn't prepared," I said, "I didn't fully understand how time-consuming and preoccupied you would be."

"Booker, if this is too much, if we can't make it because of what I've chosen to do…"

"Aubree, I acted like an asshole."

"But…"

"Let me finish before you defend me. I acted like a baby who couldn't get his way, not proud of that. Instead of staying and working things out, I left and let things fester. But I think I needed the time to figure it out in my own way. I understand what I'm getting myself into now."

"It's a lot, I realize that, but I promise to be more balanced. I've been as guilty as you have about not being open. I let my own apprehension and doubt keep me from telling you things I should be talking to you about."

"Like what?" I reached out and fingered a lock of her hair.

She frowned, brushing at my rough cheek, trying to find the right words. "I was flunking o-chem, seriously couldn't understand it, and felt like I was drowning."

"Why didn't you tell me?"

"My perfectionism reared its ugly head, and I wanted to prove I could handle it all. But in truth, I couldn't. I needed help. Thank God for my pushy friends and family. Because stupidly, I didn't think you could help... and I was embarrassed, and I didn't want to look bad in your eyes."

"Aubree, you could never do that. Sugar, we're going to promise each other right now that we'll always be honest and communicate."

She nodded. "Yes, agreed. I don't know what you were thinking and you couldn't know what I was thinking, so it's important that we not only be clear, but that we commit to staying aware of even stuff we'd rather not deal with."

"Totally, so I'm going to be honest now. Getting married is a big step for us. For me, it's a lifelong commitment. I'm pledged to you, but I'm still struggling to understand where my head is. Still trying to handle the thought of you having to juggle me in with everything else."

"I don't want to juggle you."

"I know, but it's something you're going to have to do. The workload will demand most of your time, and not just while you're becoming a doctor. Once you are a doctor, time will still be limited."

She bit her lip and closed her eyes. "Do you still want to marry me?"

I had to struggle to breathe while I pulled her against me. "Yes. I just wanted to be honest about how I feel."

"I want you to tell me how you feel. It's important. Please don't ever hold back again. I make the same promise not to, ever again. Truly, Booker. No more secrets."

I stroked her arms and down her back pulling her flush to me. So we were locked together.

"All righty now, what is this kissing game?

"It's true or false. You get the answer right and you get a kiss."

"Much better than getting pounded in the face. What's the first question?"

"Eskimo kisses are fake."

"True," I said and she kissed me.

"Kissing is like drugs."

"True. Endorphins are 200 times more powerful than drugs, and they make you giddy."

"Smart guy," she said, pulling me in for another kiss. This one lasted a little longer. I hitched Aubree higher up on my hips, making her gasp and me groan in frustration.

"Yeah, know that from running." I grinned.

"Philematology is the science of kissing."

"True...philo, phil, phila, and phile mean love."

"You are the astronaut of awesome."

My grin widened. "Right now, I'm the rocket man," I said and she smiled, and the spark that flared in her eyes unraveled me. My world lived in those eyes.

Ah, Brax, you knew what the hell you were talking about. The details, man, how did I miss them?

"Did you know that lips are sensitive?" I brushed back her hair. "That's true. Lips and fingertips are the most sensitive parts of our bodies due to the large number of nerves." I kissed her, the game forgotten. "Like playing music," I murmured and kissed her again, deeply, sucking her tongue. "Touching," I ran my fingertips over her face. "So when the fingers come into contact with the mouth..." I traced my thumb over her lower lip, her breathing shallow now, "...double sensory overload."

She moved restlessly against me and we fit together just as nature and God intended. I was lost in the storm of her body, rolling over me with thunder and lightning. Heavy, nourishing rains that filled the cavernous well inside me. Somewhere in the recesses of what was left of my mind, the tenderness, the vulnerability that I had never allowed myself found me. Regardless of what she said, I would still be her knight when she needed me. I would be anything she needed. But after Brax's pep talk, and her attempt to piss me off, I wouldn't avoid my negative feelings any more. They were all her, wrapped up in this beautiful redheaded package that I would continue to unwrap for the rest of the days I drew breath.

She laid claim to my panting mouth as my body knew hers, an intimate madness, a rollicking recklessness, a consuming joy as our souls recognized each other through the joining of our bodies. With them we could make life and with them we created a whole universe with a bang that rocked us into the cosmos.

After we came down to earth there was a lot of kissing and touching as we ate dinner, then slept close together. The days passed in a whirlwind until it was time to get dressed and go to the rehearsal dinner, run through the ceremony. At the church steps, I kissed Aubree goodbye as she went off with River.

#

Booker

The next morning I got to the church very early. I had this burning need to talk to Aubree, but of course it was bad luck to see the bride before the wedding. I was feeling like a complete jerk while all the guys got dressed in one of the rooms in the back of the church. Verity's father was officiating, and he stopped in to see how I was doing.

Before I knew what was happening I spilled my guts to him. It all came pouring out, and I was furious with myself for not seeing it sooner.

Reverend Fairchild, as calm as you please, reached out and clasped my shoulder. "I can't tell you whether to marry Aubree or not. That is your decision, Booker. But what I can tell you is you need to search deep into your heart and your mind about what you can give to this woman. Pledge everything or walk away. There are no half measures when it comes to marriage."

When he left, it was time to go to the altar, and I went with my brothers, who were both acting as my best man.

Suddenly I was struck with a burning need. I had to see Aubree, talk to her, before we said our vows.

#

Aubree

My heart was breaking as I looked at myself in the mirror while River Pearl did my hair. I felt incomplete about our talk yesterday, and felt as if I was going to break into a million pieces.

"You look, beautiful, Aubree. I'm ready to set in the veil."

"Wait," I blurted out and her hands froze.

"You don't want the veil?"

100

"Yes, I want the veil. Attach it," I said impatiently. "Then I need to see Booker."

"What? *Now*? The ceremony is about to start in like two minutes."

"Yes, River, now. I have to see him before I say my vows to him."

She set the veil and left the room. I got up, unable to breathe sitting down, and paced.

My thoughts and my excitement and anticipation hadn't let me sleep last night. I would be joining my life with Booker's, and I was still plagued by a nagging, despairing worry. Not that I was making a mistake, but that what I wanted to do with my life was going to destroy what I had with him, no matter how much we talked about it.

#

Booker

I looked at Brax, and he closed his eyes, knowing immediately that I was about to do something crazy. Then I saw River Pearl walking briskly up the aisle. She came to me and leaned in close. "Aubree needs to see you. Now. She's pretty distraught. Is everything okay, Booker?"

"It will be," I said.

Without another word, I hurried to the back of the church. When I got to Aubree's dressing room door, I knocked, my chest tight.

The door opened slightly and she said, "Booker, don't come in. You can't see me, but I have to talk to you." She took a shaky breath and said. "I can't do this."

I was confident she was not talking about marrying me. I was secure in my trust in her. "What?" I growled. "Talk to me, sugar."

"Marrying you is the only thing I'm certain about. I don't want to be a doctor if that means I'm going to lose you. It's not worth it. You are everything to me, and I want to be honest with you about this. I'll give it up. I'll figure something else out."

Everything coalesced for me in that one moment of her willingness to sacrifice her passion for me.

"Aubree, I ran from what I thought was neglect on your part. Ran from the pain of thinking that you aren't as invested in me as I am in you. But what I hadn't seen were the small things you'd done every day to keep us together. Always kissing me before you left. Leaving me little notes on my computer screen, making the time we did spend together as rich as possible."

I put my hand in my pocket and squeezed the post-it there that had been left on my pillow. A simple I love you with the o drawn as a heart. "I had been blinded by my own need to have choices. To be open to opportunities. But I see now that my choice is clear. There was nothing but one choice. Breaking it off with you is impossible, inconsolable, and not ever going to happen."

"Booker," she whispered, tears clogging her voice.

I would become the man she needed me to be. The man I was shaping into because of her molding hands, her love, her trust, and her undying hope.

Because she was everything. The only person who could break my unbreakable spirit. She was the beam of steel that ran through the core of me, bolstered me.

"I'm opening myself, right here and now, to all *your* possibilities." Decided once and for all that being her man, her bad boy Outlaw, was all that mattered. Whatever she had to do, she would do it with my love and support. This Outlaw was all in for the ride of his life.

"I will be there for you when you have to get up at three in the morning on a call, or when you couldn't make it for dinner, or cancelled a vacation, or broke our date night plans. It won't always be easy. I'm not downplaying that. But it will be worthwhile, and life, like our love, is just plain chaotic. It's still a perfect mess."

"I love you, Booker, and I can't wait to marry you."

Dr. Rust had it perfectly right. Aubree was a healer. She was a talented, brilliant, beautifully flawed woman. She was *my* healer, my heart, and without her there was no way for me to pump blood, fill my lungs, breathe.

"I am going to say my vows with complete and utter honesty. I want to marry you, too, Aubree because you are my choice. I won't force you to choose between your two loves." I wanted to support her as she grew into a complete woman, my woman, my bad-ass doctor wife, and the mother of my children.

"Close your eyes," she whispered. She waited a beat and said, "Are they closed?"

"Yes," I whispered back. I heard the rustle of cloth and the squeak of the door. Then I felt the warm press of her lips against mine. I kissed her back with all my passion and love.

I couldn't live with anything less.

And I couldn't live without her.

#

Aubree

I broke the kiss and looked up at him, the tender look on his face, even with his eyes closed, making me go all weak and warm. The last thing I wanted to do was let this moment go, but I had little choice. We were getting married, and we'd have a lifetime of these moments. I ran my hand up his rib cage in a long caress, then reluctantly stepped back out of his arms.

"Get to the altar. I'll be right there."

I slipped back into the room and closed the door. I checked the mirror, and, yes, the tears had wreaked havoc with my makeup. I did a quick patch job, picked up my beautiful bouquet, and turned toward the door. Right outside, Mike, my stepdaddy, stood in his tux.

"Is everything worked out?"

I smiled from ear to ear. All my concerns gone. "Yes, totally."

He offered me his arm. "Good. Your mother was getting worried when Booker left."

"We just needed a few more minutes together."

He led me to the entrance to the church, and as soon as I became visible, everyone turned. The organ started to play, but it was cut short by Booker's voice singing the opening words to "I'll Be." He'd made that our song that long-ago day at the barbeque just after our mutual declaration of love.

I stopped in my tracks and took a breath, my throat thickening with the emotions I was trying to keep under control. Booker left the altar, still singing, his powerful voice echoing throughout the church.

When he got to the chorus, he set his hand on his heart, looking so handsome and sexy in his tux. He stopped, closing his eyes and belting out the words, his hands forming into fists, as the emotion he was feeling came through his voice. Then he continued to move down the aisle, singing all the way.

When he reached me, Mike stepped back, and Booker cupped my face and sang the second chorus. Then he tucked my arm into his, and we started to walk. About halfway down the aisle, those words resonating in me, he twirled me. At the head of the aisle, he stopped, turned me and finished out the song while he held my gaze.

As the last words to the song echoed in the church, I

whispered, "That was beautiful."

"You are beautiful, stunning. Let's go tie the damn knot," he laughed softly.

He gave me back to Mike and went and took his place. There wasn't a dry eye in the church.

Booker, my unpredictable Outlaw.

The ceremony went by so fast, and the reception was in full swing when I finally got up the courage to check my grades. When I saw my o-chem grade I breathed a sigh of relief. Booker, who was looking over my shoulder, smiled and nuzzled my neck. "A minus. Will that do?"

"That will do," I said.

"So, after DC—"

"DC?"

"Yeah, I hope you wrote your speech."

"It's written," I said, sliding my finger along his jaw. "How did you know?"

"Dr. Palmer sent an email to that wily Dr. Rust. He was the one who told me, and I don't want you to miss out. I've always wanted to tour the White House."

"Holy cow. I better alert the authorities. Mr. Outlaw Goes to Washington!"

"Hey, you." He knuckled my head.

"Where are we going for our honeymoon?"

He looked down and toyed with my wedding band. "How does Tanzania sound?"

"East Africa?"

"Yeah, it isn't exactly a honeymoon at first."

"What do you mean? I want a honeymoon with *you*, Booker. I want to keep you in bed for a week, for the rest of the summer."

He gave me a wicked grin. "I endorse that," he whispered, "But first I booked you into a pre-medical shadowing program for two weeks. It's in Tanzania. Afterwards, we can have our honeymoon there, or we can go somewhere else. You tell me where you want to go."

"No." My heart swelled and his words came back to me. *I'm opening myself right here and now to all* your *possibilities*. He was true to his word, had been true to me even when we were still struggling with our own issues.

"What?"

I smiled. "Unbook it. I'll go overseas for that kind of thing next year."

"Are you serious?"

"Heart attack serious.' I wiggled my brows. "Right now, I'm eager to get to the wedding night and you out of that tux."

"Me too, sugar. Me too. That laced up thing you've got going in the back has been driving me crazy all day."

I cupped the back of his head and we didn't need any clinking champagne glasses to indulge in a kiss. "I do love the idea of the shadowing program, Booker. Thank you for your thoughtfulness. Elephants and zebras are nice and all, but they can wait. If I have a choice, I would have to say Paris."

"Whatever you want, Mrs. Outlaw," he said with another wicked grin.

We devoured Brax's food, prepared to perfection as usual, and people were raving over Brax's cakes. I had two helpings—after all, he did say he took all the calories out. As the reception began to wind down, I rose and moved between Boone and Brax, who were sitting next to us, grasping them both around their shoulders, hugging them tight. "I love you guys," I whispered.

"Well, isn't this a freaking love fest," Brax replied and I laughed.

Boone said, "Welcome to the family, Breebree."

I kissed them both, hugged my best friends, and sat

back down close to Booker.

He leaned over and said, "Now you're an Outlaw, too."

I smiled, kissed him hard on the mouth while everyone whooped, and said against his lips. "Well, that's just fucking perfect."

Zoe Dawson

EPILOGUE

Aubree

I STOOD next to the altar while my momma-in-law and Winchester Sutton took their vows. She was dressed in the beautiful off-white dress that all of us girls pitched in to sew for her. Verity was such an amazing designer. I looked out in the crowd to see Minnie and Deke, holding hands, her head on his broad shoulder. I wondered how much longer it was going to be before we had another wedding on our hands.

Rory and Savannah were sitting next to them, looking just as happy and contented. Who would beat who to the altar?

My momma had been Evie's choice for matron of honor and, River Pearl, Verity and I stood up with her as her bridesmaids. Her sons were ushers, while James Sutton acted as Win's best man.

It was a balmy day in October, and Booker and I were working every day to stay connected. I was ramping up for my MCAT testing, and Booker was helping me study, quizzing me when he wasn't busy distracting me with his astronaut of awesome routine. Stress still played a part in causing some minor squabbles and it wasn't always paradise, but it was real, disarming, fulfilling, and, as usual, darned messy.

The summer had gone by way to fast, but it had given Booker and me enough time and privacy to reconnect. I was rejuvenated by his love and passion, the trip to DC, our honeymoon in Paris, so romantic. He had sweet-talked me into a shadowing experience in Tanzania and it turned out to be far more than I could possibly have imagined. After it was over, Booker joined me, and we spent another two weeks there, going on safari, taking in the stunning views of Mt. Kilimanjaro, encountering the interesting tribal cultures, and enjoying the warm, sandy beaches. It was wonderful.

Booker had finished his first Outlaw Legacy book, which told Duel, Amy, and the Colonel's story with passion and wonderful characterizations. After River Pearl read the final draft, she hugged Booker with tears because he'd portrayed her ancestor, not as a depraved thief and murderer, but as a man driven by his needs, torn, and then devastated by the harm he'd caused. I was so proud of him.

Who knew how critics and readers would receive it, but I sensed it was going to have a wonderful reception, and his fans would be thrilled.

After the ceremony, we ended up at Evie and Win's. They were going on their honeymoon the next day, but wanted a family celebration tonight.

I heard Booker groan when I saw Boone with a jar of fruit punch moonshine, toting a Monopoly board game under his arm.

Boone cleared his throat portentously. "The word is 'go.' Every time someone says go, we drink."

"Set up the board," Brax said, "and I'm watching you, Ma. You always have an abundance of pink fifties."

She laughed. "Are you saying that I'm a cheater?"

"If the pink fifty fits..." We all laughed, and I went to make sure there was enough pain reliever in the medicine cabinet.

It rained all the way home and, of course, leaving Suttontowne was always difficult, but in the morning after our crazy, drunk, barely-remembered Monopoly game, we were quite blissfully happy.

Since Evie couldn't resist looking for things when she went antiquing, she sent me home with a vintage clock I set on the mantle while Booker carried in a gorgeous chest, raindrops clinging to his hair and jacket, moisture slicking his skin. He glanced at me, his expression unreadable. "Is there enough wood, or do I need to bring some more in?"

I shook my head, "No. The wood box is full."

He went back outside, and I stared at the empty doorway, wondering at his pensiveness. I shucked my jacket and went into the kitchen to start some coffee brewing and get out cups.

Booker returned with two more boxes of dishes that Evie had found, and I was thrilled with the pattern. Booker picked up my jacket as he passed and hung both his and mine by the door. He walked over to the fireplace and began to lay the fire while the scent of freshly brewed French Vanilla flavored the air.

I poured two cups, the gurgling blending with the crackle and snap from the brightly burning fire. Booker was standing near the windows looking out at the rain, his hands in the back pockets of his jeans.

I watched him, the warmth of my love stronger and deeper than the fire could ever penetrate, the dark beauty of him setting off a wild flutter in my chest. We had overcome some heavy duty feelings and emotions, made monumental decisions, and were weathering the storm of working side by side for our future.

I set the cups down on the coffee table and crossed the room. He was lost in thought. I wrapped my arms around him and he sighed. "What are you thinking so hard about?"

He stared out, the muscle in his jaw tensing, his expression going tender. His jaw flexed; then he answered. "Ma."

I ran my hands up his waist, one settling on his chest where I could feel the strong beat of his heart.

"I had no idea that everything was going to turn out this way. Back when I was loving you from afar, I was miserable. Unrequited love is so painful. But then we found each other, overcame our bullshit, and are now married."

His hands covered mine. "Boone and Brax..."

"Yeah, they are pretty situated. You know it's just a matter of time before Brax falls."

"Falls," I said. "Like getting married dumps you in a ditch or a pit?"

He laughed, and the sound of it was like music.

"No, falling, as in not having a choice because there is nothing you can do but open your arms and embrace the air and the impact when you hit."

I pressed my cheek to his back, breathing him in.

I went to turn away and grab up my MCAT book, but Booker caught my wrist, palm sliding against palm as he gripped my hand. The instant his fingers slid through mine, I understood what he needed, and I closed my eyes against the wild surge of emotion that made me shiver.

I needed to study, but this time out of time with Booker now automatically made me shift my schedule. In the past, I would have protested, but my newfound confidence, and my promise, shifted everything. With a low moan, I turned blindly into his arms, sliding my hands up his back and holding him close. For several heartbeats, he looked into my eyes, taking me in, while I absorbed our closeness, our physical touch, our need and desire for each other.

A Perfect Wedding

He caught me against him in a viselike embrace, emitting a ragged groan as he found my mouth with a kiss that shattered my senses. His hand supporting the back of my head, he locked his other arm around my hips, hauling me up against him. His mouth opened hungrily against mine, feeding the need that raged in him, it was in the flavor of his kiss.

And then passion claimed us, consumed us, pulling us under, the fire fusing us into one.

Awareness returned in fragments—like slivers of light infiltrating my mind—and I tightened my arms around him, twisting my face against his damp neck, the softness of the large array of throw pillows beneath me and his weight on top of me the only reality.

A tremor coursed through me, the rush of emotion so intense it was almost unbearable, and I clenched my jaw against it. God, but I loved this man. So much. So very much. Drawing a deep, painful breath, I slid my hand up the back of his neck, cradling his head against me with infinite tenderness. Booker shuddered and pressed his face against the curve of my shoulder, his hold on me tightening convulsively. I closed my eyes, waiting for the ache of emotion to ease a little; then I stroked his head and pressed a tender kiss against his neck.

Booker raised his head and looked at me, his blue, oh-so-blue eyes filled with such intense, unguarded emotion they made my heart contract all over again.

I smiled at him as I gently caressed his scratchy face. "See? Told you these throw pillows would come in handy."

He laughed and nuzzled and blew on my neck until I squealed. "You were right. Let's run out and get some more. Spread them all through the house. Then we'll always have a soft place to land."

I dug into his ribs at his sarcastic tone, and he jerked

and made the cutest laugh noise.

"Seriously, it's time we stopped fooling around and get back to your da-da-da-daaaaa, dreaded MCATs."

"Are you always going to say that with a drumroll?"

"Yes, it needs music of its own."

"Come on. So far they haven't been bad."

"That's because you are so damned smart."

I dug in his ribs again, but the wily Outlaw blocked me, and it was he who got to my ribs. I went crazy wiggling and giggling beneath him.

"Oooh, keep doing that, and we'll be heading upstairs for round two, my sexy redhead."

"You are a wicked, bad boy."

"Only when it comes to you and your delicious body." His chest expanded, and he slid his arms around me and held me fiercely, protectively, surrounding me all over again with his deep, abiding love.

"Geezus, I love you, Aubree."

His voice was so full of emotion, it was impossible to say more. I closed my eyes and turned my face against his neck, holding him just as fiercely, as protectively as he was holding me.

After a moment, he sighed. "Okay, I got your next test question."

I sighed right back at him.

"All right, I'm ready."

"It's an essay."

"I'm Hemingway when it comes to essays."

"Oh, the girl shoots and scores, because she's got game."

"Ha! What is the question, Quiz Master?"

"Explain what you think the following statement means: How do you feel about our sex life lately?"

I burst out laughing. "That is not an MCAT question! You silly man."

He gave me a mock serious look, his blue eyes full of

equally mock innocence. "Totally a question. You have to answer it."

"Do, I?"

"Yes. And I have follow-up questions."

"Oh God, my stomach hurts from laughing. You are so bad."

His face went soft. "I can be badder....and that means oh-so-good."

"Well," I slipped my hand down his body and cupped him. "I've been thinking I have something I want to do with my hot, wet mouth that my wonderful, sweet husband will love."

When I stroked him, he started to get hard, then when I ran my palm over the tip of him, he groaned.

I licked his neck and bit him, and his breathing speeded up. Pushing him onto his back, I bent down.

"You have those questions fully formed," I said, then gave him what he and I wanted.

His voice was ragged when he said, "I'll work...oh shit...on them later.

And, we did, until we got hungry and went out to dinner. As we settled in at our table and I picked up the menu, then dropped it and looked at Booker. "Just so you know, I'm so eating whatever dessert you order."

The rich laughter of my gorgeous, unpredictable, smarty-pants Outlaw husband was all mine...for ever after.

****

COME BACK TO HOPE PARISH...

The stories in Hope Parish continue with Boone and Verity Outlaw as they struggle with a shocking and heart-wrenching remnant from their past. Is their relationship strong enough to weather this upheaval? You're all invited to an Outlaw Holiday. Come back to Hope Parish for the release of *A Perfect Holiday*!